Rites of Passage

Rites of Passage

Darryl Lauster

Creators Publishing
Hermosa Beach, CA

RITES OF PASSAGE

COPYRIGHT © 2017 DARRYL LAUSTER

Cover art Lynda White
Creative Coordinator Peter Kaminski

CREATORS PUBLISHING
737 3rd St
Hermosa Beach, CA 90254
310-337-7003

Library of Congress Control Number: 2017941109
ISBN (print): 9781945630606
ISBN (ebook): 9781945630361

First Edition
Printed in the United States of America
1 3 5 7 9 10 8 6 4 2

*The bulk of this novel was written
during residencies at
The Byrdcliffe Art Colony
and
The Vermont Studio Center*

~~~

It is dedicated to my wife

~~~

Contents

One

John Diver led an extraordinarily average life. In this he was no different than the vast bulk of humanity. Eat. Drink. Piss. Shit. Rinse. Repeat. But what separated John from others was his complete recognition of this reality. He understood that once gone, there would be little by which to remember him, that death would wipe the earth of his memory. He understood this, and yet plodded on, a willing participant in a human experiment he could not ascertain, but to which he simply acquiesced. In the absence of a reason there seemed little else to do.

Diver held this point dear—that such an awareness was valuable, even if it afforded little usefulness. He believed in two primary human afflictions. The first is powerlessness. But the second, and by far the worse, is ignorance. And that which Diver held most dear was his belief that life, at least for the masses, was a truce between middling wretchedness and a quest for intimacy. Sex, it seemed, afforded not only a respite from suffering, but it allowed people the illusion of immortality by progeny, and of being remembered by a future someone that shared some part of him or herself.

Diver enjoyed the peace and quiet of being alone. He drank almost daily. Just enough so, in addition to Lexapro, he could keep his anxiety at bay. When he did sleep, he had nightmares of demons. But despite his lackluster physicality he kept his mind sharp. It was the sharpest tool his body carried, and he did work to keep it honed.

But this is not to say that he was a confident man. He often flashed back to the ninth grade. Photography class. His eye was good. His compositions, always off-center and focused on nondescript environments, had caught the eye of his classmates. But his grades were poor. He hung with the delinquents, long hair covering their eyes, black T-shirts bearing Black Sabbath and Iron Maiden tour dates. They would sit in the back of the room, snapping blurry pictures of their middle fingers rising up in a gesture of what they thought was defiance but was actually a poverty of ideas Diver remembered the day Mr. Dworkin, his art teacher, pulled him aside after class. "John," he said, "You have talent, but you need to learn how to pick your friends."

What did it mean? Did he know that these were the only friends John had? Did he presume there were other better friends-to-be lying in wait that John ignored? It was impossible to know, but John took it to mean that he was damaged, lacking in completeness somehow, and that he did not belong.

Such thoughts engrossed him most mornings when peeling asparagus…or dicing onions…or skimming the raft of a well-prepared consommé. Diver was the co-owner/chef of his town's only vegetarian restaurant, *De Terre,* now in its third year of business. His ten-tabled, three-employeed venture had passed the test of time — at least the time in which most restaurants go under — to assemble a small, eclectic but erudite clientele of regulars. He made little money after all bills were paid, but it afforded him solace and a bounty of time to think. And when he desired conversations beyond those with his vegetables, he needn't go further than the nearest four-top in the dining room.

Food was not his first endeavor. He had an advanced degree in art history from Delhi, which was a useful as glass hammer. As a younger student, Diver had a voracious appetite for the humanities—philosophy and history mainly, but he found comfort in the fact that art was the first language—and began doctoral studies in Neolithic iconography. His dissertation proposed a funerary connection between Cycladic figures and Egyptian Ka statuary, but like many things in his life, it was never completed. There was a certain point, one evening, buried deep in scholastic treatises, impassively searching for a document on ancient diorite quarries when it hit him.

He had stopped caring.

And so cooking became a new release. It afforded a perfect mixture of quietude and concentration. A place where not belonging was irrelevant. Alone, behind his line, camouflaged with an arsenal of stainless steel utensils, Diver could master a craft by uniting the formulaic with the creative. Slowly, recipe books replaced art journals. Béchamels replaced flash drives. And after paying his dues behind the lines for several years, he found it difficult to continue working in busy restaurants. Drugs were rampant. Noise destroyed focus. Speed devoured precision. There was a moment when it all seemed to come together—one of those moments that made it seem like there is a plan to one's existence. There was an empty building. There was a credit union. There was a down payment. *De Terre* was born. Diver had a purpose. If cooking was not the world's oldest profession, then it certainly was the noblest.

Feed them first, then ask of them virtue…

Of course, Diver knew that his decision to become a restaurateur was not as impulsive as one might think. He sometimes indulged himself as an irrational romantic, one who had faith in humanity but still wanted a good distance from it. Graduate school had much in common with a kitchen. One spends the majority of one's day working alone for the ultimate benefit of the interested few, if any. The higher one climbed up the academic ladder, the more removed one was from the rest of world. This pleased him greatly, even though he was far from the highest rungs. His particular position obliged him a general concern for the masses without the messiness of having to interact with them.

But this is not to say he ever felt himself particularly significant.

In fact, the only trait Diver felt he brought to the table was his ability to set it — that is, to create a space where people could be thoughtful, be together and be present. And if they could not act like assholes for an hour or so, that was gravy...

His favorite part of any month was its final week. It was this week that Diver would prepare to change his menu, as he had done habitually for the last three years. By now there were favorites finding their way frequently into his selections, but for the most part he attempted to embody a seasonal culinary vision. This humble renewal, this gastronomic monthly renaissance, was as close to baptism as Diver would ever get. This month was particularly distinctive. It was the beginning of fall. The harvest moon. Victory of the root vegetable. Ascension of the gourd.

If our fates were to be lives etched in distress and anonymity, then at least we could enjoy a good meal now and then.

But that, too, required work. Diver had just begun the day.

And work required tools.

A well-balanced knife is a work of art. In the proper hands it cuts almost imperceptibly, evidenced solely by the rap of its heel against a polypropylene board. Diver had two favorites: a twelve-inch Hoffritz French knife and an eight-inch scalloped boner, maker unknown, but an old-school double-riveted European standard for sure. The Germans and the Japanese made the best steel, but Diver preferred the heft of German blades to the svelte precision of Japanese models. The twelve-inch would be considered too long by many, less fit for chiffonades or garnishing, but for Diver it was beautifully practical, a workhorse at piercing, cleaving and dicing alike. It was the perfect instrument for his current autumnal task — disemboweling pumpkin.

As he felt the weight of the tang in his palm, he could not help but think that such an object would be illegal on the street, with its fixed blade far longer than the lawful four inches. Were it an AR-15 or a Glock it would be perfectly fine, draped on his body like a scarf or cellphone. But in their collective wisdom, legislators had recognized a single-edged blade as being far too dangerous for open carry. Killing with a gun was cultured. J. M. Coetzee had described guns in his first novella as the difference between savages and civilized men. With a knife, you had to get close, feel the pressure of the skin release as you pushed deep, feel the resistance of a bone, hear one's breath grow wet with blood. With a gun, you just closed your eyes and pulled the trigger, from distance, waiting only for your subsequent news interview to tidy things up. Only the survivor got to tell the story. This was the new Wild West.

Obsession with the Second Amendment combined two very real but very unspoken realities. Firstly, that most people are in great need of overcompensating for their failings. A handgun is the only real cock many men have ever held. Secondly, that somewhere under all of our denials is the recognition that life is cheap. Like rats, the human race has bred itself incessantly into a population crisis, wherein competition turns to violence. Guns are meant to kill. And since we have little success against the bacteria, viruses and cancers that cull our numbers, they are how we eradicate the next biggest problem — each other. As a nation, we had made peace with the occasional mass murder as a trade-off for wanting to play with our toys. It was the American way.

Mornings are the best time to prepare dinner. One's head is clear, waked to life with the heady aroma of rich ground coffee. The world is quiet, studying the day to come. It was between eight o'clock and noon that Diver got his best work done, starting with the typical necessities, a court bouillon, fresh pasta, and washed greens. The mise en place would follow, and then it was all business. Deliveries arrived between nine and eleven — a local organic co-op dropped that day's star attraction — and Diver smiled at the crate of waxy white cushaws at his feet.

Most bake the gourd before gathering its flesh, which after cooking, is easily massaged from the skin in steamy spoonfuls of pulp. This imparts a richer and deeper flavor, particularly if baked in a wood oven. It also alleviates the difficulty of cutting it raw, which can be a difficult task. But the Hoffritz was made for this, and Diver cleaved the blond body into uniform six-inch sections deftly. Baking was not an option here; he needed his pumpkin poached in stock — the only appropriate beginning for the subtle fragrant bisque he desired.

His stock was simple but well-rounded: two gallons of filtered water brought slowly to simmer with fresh elephant garlic, shallots, fennel, carrots, and celery. Add one cup of riesling and two tablespoons of honey. Into this, three stems of fresh thyme, lavender and marjoram, one bay leaf, and white pepper. Forty minutes on the stovetop, no more. Strain through a chinois. Diver had doubled his recipe that day, reserving half the broth for soup and pasta, and reducing the remainder into a richer base for glazes and beurre blancs. Soon, his favorite kettle was alive with bobbing amber rafts floating atop the aromatic liquid.

Kant's *Critique of Reason* dissects the concept of judgment into four discrete units. His consequent theories on the intersections of genius and taste with respect to the beautiful and the sublime withstanding, Diver had always felt that Kant's first throwaway category — that of the agreeable, to have been too quickly forsaken. For Kant, this judgment was purely sensory, based on one's inclination. Presumably, its lack of universal possibility made it unattractive. Kant assumed that *agreeableness* lay in one's perception of a thing, and not the thing in itself. This supposes the reason that many find broccoli delicious and many don't, Diver presumed. The broccoli was consistent; one's sensory affinities were the variant. Since there was no universal accord on broccoli (had one escaped him?), Diver never pressed the issue with his patrons. But he felt the urge to stand up for chefs everywhere. Was there a genius to cooking broccoli in the way that genius is identified in the sculpting of Michelangelo's *David*? There were pratfalls to this argument, to which Diver found himself engrossed yet again while staring at the half-empty quart of heavy cream in his walk-in.

For Kant, cooking was not an art per se, because all art must contain within it a quality of resolution without the appearance of labor. This definition holds up well in the contemporary world, very well in fact, and is possibly his most poetic reference to art making in general. After all, a steak is done when it is done. It is the product of a recognized interim of work: five minutes of grill time for rare, eight minutes for medium, etc. And its labor can be easily instructed, understood, and repeated. Recalling that Kant's sensory reference was to the eater, as opposed to the preparer, the question that remained was whether broccoli could ever be more than the sum of its parts, or whether a meal, prepared with genius, could transform a judgment of taste.

Now that the cushaw was nicely poached, Diver ladled the pieces into a food processor, with a small amount of the stock, and puréed the mixture together for several minutes after having shaved a slight pinch of fresh nutmeg into the base. He returned this blend back into the remainder of the stock and poured again through the chinois. It was then time to turn to the stovetop to prepare a roux.

Roux is one of the most personalized mediums in the chef's toolkit. It is prepared an innumerable manner of ways, each with different ingredients and different processes. Diver utilized three most often; two stovetop preparations and one baked in the oven. This roux, which necessitated a buttery lightness, was a simple one that required little more than patience and attention, two things that Diver had always humorously noted were missing in a great majority of human relationships. Of course, a relationship with butter would always be more rewarding than a relationship with another person. As he stirred a small handful of sifted flour into his skillet of softly melted butter, Diver smiled, watching the compound bubble over the low heat. Twenty minutes of gentle massaging later the soup would finally begin.

Returning the puréed base to the gentle heat of a steam kettle, Diver added one strand of saffron and enough roux to thicken the mixture. His mind was beginning to wander, as it often did in the late morning. Philosophy never helped, he had determined, for while he enjoyed it immensely, it often left him feeling ill-equipped for the kind of deep concentration it required. Diver was a jumper — from this to that — and never thought himself the type to dedicate himself to a single endeavor over the entire course of his life. He had temporal immersions. There was Taoism, but it forbade drinking. There was painting, but it was too expensive. There was the guitar, but he had small fingers. There was poetry, but he sucked at writing.

Diver understood, quite clearly in fact, that the real reason for his lack of dedication to his former endeavors was twofold. The first was natural, he reasoned — the very human enterprise of experimentation, of finding oneself, of claiming one's identity by slowly editing out irrelevancy. It was an odd claim to self-knowledge — an affirmation of what one was not, but for the most part it seemed human enough. The other cause of his indolence was more problematic — but perhaps equally human — his penchant for using cynicism as a self-defense mechanism. It was a postmodern affliction, borne in part from certain global distresses, political corruptions, and ethical compromises, but moreover Diver had cultivated this particular personality trait like a doting shepherd, fencing in his vulnerability. He was an abject anomaly in the human disposition. When Diver found himself in danger of a certain emotional commitment to anything, a trigger within him pulled him away. One can never not belong if one never connects. From distance it became easy to dissect, to chew it up, until it held life no longer, and became a caricature for the masses.

As he creamed out the bisque, completing its preparation, Diver smiled. There would be more time for Kant later, but for now it was time for lunch, and Diver had guests arriving soon.

Two

"But Socrates was killed because he posed a threat to Athenian stability..." argued one of three men at the table. The man who spoke was the tallest, with a slight build that complemented his Scandinavian features.

William Hogue, along with his brother Jacob, ran a well-known bookstore downtown. The two were regulars at *De Terre*, and also hosted book club luncheons during the first and last weeks of the month. The word "club" was perhaps too strong. Diver never noticed more than four persons at any one meeting, although three of them seemed dedicated enough to attend regularly. Besides William and Jacob, that day's attendance included *De Terre's* other co-owner Simon Pence and an engaging young woman named Claire, who studied literature at the state university, and who had just returned from the restroom to sit down at the table midtopic.

"No. The Athenian democracy was not corrupt," replied Simon. "It was the most progressive entity of its time."

"But opposed to change, or even the kinds of questions that might beget change," added Claire, not missing a beat.

"Let's not forget that Athenian democracy by definition meant rule by men."

Diver approached the table with canapés, as was his usual contribution to the club. *De Terre* was only open for dinner, but Diver made exceptions for local groups who inquired about his space. Besides the regular book club meetings, he hosted occasional luncheons for the VFW, the local Oddfellows and even once a baby shower for a local woman named Marjorie. It was a good way to make a little extra money without too much trouble. Most often it required no extra server, as Diver put limits on the number of persons he could accommodate.

He placed a silver tray of assorted finger sandwiches down. There were wild mushroom empanadas, grilled manchego en croute, and freshly steamed edamame. Paired with the several bottles of Chimay already half-quaffed, Diver thought it a well-balanced, if not calorific, midday meal.

"John, have you read Plato's *Apology?*" asked Jacob, "Join us for a pint. This looks fantastic. Enjoy it with us."

Diver thought it odd that the invitation came from Jacob. Bill was the more outspoken of the two, and did most of the talking. Jacob was friendly enough, but always seemed to hover under his older brother's shadow.

"Thanks, Jacob," Diver replied, "I'll take you up on a quick beer, but I can't stay long. I've got a lasagna to prepare."

"So...have you read Plato?" Bill asked.

"Back in the day," Diver replied, "It's been a long time though."

"Well we're just arguing over it mostly," Claire answered. "Simon and Jacob are ready to execute him all over again..."

Simon interjected. He was a scholarly man, always well-dressed but never fussy in his appearance. Diver knew him well, and had great affection for him. In many ways, he owed his restaurant to Simon's father.

"Socrates posed questions not as a means to subvert power, but to caricature it, offering no solutions himself, no means of progress...which, of course, flies in the face of any meaningful critique."

"And, one could make an argument that he was a threat," Jacob added, "as any dissident with an audience might be. Asking certain questions can be dangerous. The first amendment is not limitless. But he does offer solutions, Simon. Just not in this book."

"I don't follow," Bill continued.

"In *The Republic* he calls it the noble lie," Jacob offered, "Socrates himself conceded that any society must be founded on some unquestionable assumption, some legitimizing foundation on which all cultural construct is built—laws, ethics, customs."

"*Nomoi,*" Diver stated in deadpan fashion.

"Nomoi?" Jacob repeated.

"It's the Greek word for customs, translated from the text," Diver explained. He didn't know why he blurted it out. He had no real desire to become part of the conversation. He was enjoying his role as observer, quickly downing half his pint of Belgian ale. After speaking, he bit his lip hard, thinking himself pretentious. The sweetness of his blood combined with the heavy caramel liquid. The pain felt good.

"See? Name another chef in town who knows ancient Greek," Bill said warmly, patting Diver on the shoulder, "So what's your take on our discussion here? How would you have voted at the trial?"

"Well," Diver started, "despite the title of the book, Socrates doesn't ever apologize. But I think he chose to die in Athens to prove a point. Perhaps it was his way of daring the government to execute a man for asking questions, which, as Jacob said, inherently proves that questions themselves can be dangerous to institutions that don't like to provide answers."

Simon looked up. "Ah, my dear John. Couldn't the question only be dangerous when asked by the wrong person?"

"Either way," Diver replied, finishing the last of his glass, "I'd have taken exile..." He wiped the froth from his lips and placed his hands on the table. "Enjoy your discussion, guys."

As he entered the kitchen he bit down on his lip again.

It's when the first warm and sweet taste of blood fills the bottom of your mouth and pools around your gums, the quick pulse of pain when your incisor rips the flesh of your cheek away, the side of your mouth feeling like uncooked hash against your tongue–these are moments of merit. It is difficult to explain to others. They feel no necessity to destroy themselves from the inside. But neither do they recognize the satisfaction of doing so. Those who will eat themselves as a result of inadequacies, of disabilities of the mind and spirit, of the flaws of conscience, of insecurity, of hypocrisy, of sloth, of wanting too much – those are the efficient ones. Save the trials and public debate for other matters. They know we are all guilty, and they await the serenity that comes from moments when exhaustion and injury position one to embrace surrender. The eyes close, you exhale, the voices go quiet and the noise stops. It's the little peace we have in this shitstorm. And if you have to hurt yourself to find it, it's the price you pay. It's a bargain really, compared to the complete ignorance of the rest of the world.

As he returned to the solitude of the kitchen Diver noticed the ventilation grates, now in need of a thorough cleaning, glistening above his Garland range. To be exiled, he thought, was it such a punishment at all? Surely more difficult in the ancient world, he noted, where one's food could not be ordered from a menu so easily. Beyond that, of the many notable exiles he could recall, so many misanthropes, was it not a reward of its own kind? Ovid, Dante, Courbet — Diver could only imagine the special privilege of being cast out of the society one so harshly, and so beautifully, rebelled against. Was it not a vindication? Was it not a reward granted for the hardships of communing with such wasted life — life not only *not* worth living, as Socrates had stated, but also not worth living amongst?

Long ago he had read an Edward Said essay, which described exile as an "unhealable rift between a human being and a native place, between the self and its true home." Diver thought this a warning against too romantic a view of expulsion, a view that saw one's life as a kind of profligate Jataka tale. But Said's view was equally romantic, he thought, erroneously based on the idea that the self had a home to be torn from. That such a thing as a native place existed. It recognized the reality of nurture supplanting nature, and the synchronicity between culture and geography, but forsook the inherent alienation somehow encoded into human identity. "We are unknown to ourselves, we knowers…" begins Nietzsche's *On the Genealogy of Morality*, a text Diver slogged through for several undergraduate seminars, but had always remembered its wonderfully enigmatic opening line. What was Nietzsche's game? Are we truly alien to ourselves? Surely this would explain the success of advertising — and its ability to define the masses by need. If need, in that context, could be defined by a lack of self-knowledge, then identity in the 21st century could be characterized more appropriately through repeated clothing purchases than through family trees.

This, of course, was no great revelation. America, it could be argued, was never a native place to begin with. Having begun from the noblest intentions, its founders could not anticipate an indigenous populace who believed themselves sovereign even before America had birthed herself as a rogue post-colonial nation. In fact, history could be equally argued as the codified and systematic displacement of humans through time. Cyclical waves of forced migration defined the human situation. Sumer, Akkad, Nubia, Punt, Canaan, Judea. We have been exiled since Eden, destined to wander as Noah, as Amhose, as Moses, Odysseus, Aeneus, and Siddhartha. If we are unknown to ourselves, surely we are not foreign to a ten-thousand-year pattern of human exodus. It extends like a snake through time, and we, riding for a short time on a single coil, are able to see neither its head nor tail.

Exile. Our destiny.

Diver finished placing the porcelain cups on a flat serving tray, having ladled five ounces of pumpkin bisque in each. He topped the hot soup with a garnish of crème fraiche and a single chive. After adding a shallow dish of oyster crackers, he brought the tray up to his shoulder and returned to his dining room.

Jacob was talking as Diver approached the table. "I thought you'd enjoy a preview of this month's soup," he offered, placing the tray down on the table, now filled with empty pint glasses, necklaces of foam still clinging to their walls.

"It smells delicious," said Claire, wafting the steam from her cup to her nose.

"John's soup is always the best thing on the menu," Bill followed, grabbing a spoon from the table. He gingerly dipped the flatware into the broth and brought it to his lips, blowing gently, before a passable slurp.

"Oh, very nice."

Bill ate at *De Terre* several times per month, typically on Fridays, and often with Jacob and Jacob's wife, Nancy. Having divorced several years ago, Diver noted that he seemed never to bring a date of his own to the restaurant, even though he was a successful and handsome man. Diver wondered if it wasn't his beard, now grown almost to Marx-like dimensions that kept him uncoupled. Nevertheless, Bill was an excellent guest, and did provide warmth to the room whenever he entered. Diver liked having him there, even if always at arms length. He found him a comfortable presence.

"The funny thing is," Bill continued, "I thought I'd drop some weight coming here. Clean out the plumbing as they say. Eat more vegetables. More fiber. Of course, John's cooking has added two sizes to my belt."

"It's god's little joke," replied Jacob, "at the time of our greatest intellectual productivity, we are in our physical decline."

"You're both spring chickens," entered Simon, "barely out of your first colonoscopies."

"Simon," Claire interrupted, "that's as far as I want to take that visual." Then changing the subject, she turned to John. "John, oh! Look at your lip. It's swollen."

"I banged it earlier."

"Ouch. Do I taste nutmeg in this?"

"Yes. And some sherry to pick it up," Diver answered. He noticed that she had become more comfortable with her mostly male group.

"Let's return to the book," Bill offered, enjoying his bisque, "but to a different subject now. Let's talk of this *daimonion* — it seems the prototype of what we might call conscience."

"Perhaps," Jacob answered, "or is it Plato's strategic deflector, an excuse for his insolence. Like that witch he talked about...what was her name? Does anyone here think she even existed?"

"Of course she did. Who but a woman to teach a man about love?" Claire added seductively.

At that point Diver withdrew from the group, politely bidding they enjoy the remainder of their soups. While he enjoyed Plato, he desired his return to exile.

There was something comfortable about being in his kitchen. Something safe and prideful. Of course, he wasn't completely alone. He had his satellite radio, a luxury he could not imagine living without. He listened almost exclusively to talk radio, the political shows, and even sports news. It kept the day going, particularly in the late afternoons when he always lost steam. And there was Lanny, his longtime waiter. A very good waiter, by John's measure. Diver had worked with him now for two years and considered him an asset, particularly after his prior server, a college student named Yvette. That experience had ended so badly he referred to her afterward only as *the mistake*. Lanny came in about four most nights, set the tables and tidied the small but discriminating bar before opening the doors at five-thirty.

Diver looked up at the clock, noting it would be about an hour before Lanny came in. Exile lite, he thought, perhaps that's what I'm looking for.

Three

A good cassoulet should be a mainstay on most menus. It's incredibly versatile yet familiar, invoking childhood memories of cold nights in the country, and the humble ubiquity of the wooden spoon. Diver had about five such rotational dishes that he highlighted on his menu, each changing with the season. In the spring, he offered green beans and field onions in a tomato concassé. Summer meant green tomatoes with okra and garlic. Fall brought the mushroom into play. Of course, due to their lack of meat, Diver's dishes were not traditional in the southern French history of the dish, although he believed in staying as true as possible to its peasant origins.

Diver brought to his nose a plump morel from the shallow cardboard crate. He avoided allowing his fungi to touch metal, particularly in storage, and asked his purveyors to do the same. Most of his staple produce came locally from nearby farmers during the growing seasons. He even advertised local orchards on his menu, believing it to be both good business and good ethics. But just as often than not, he relied on California for the bulk of his nongreens. The morels had just arrived, quite costly, but worth every penny. Their flavor was mellow and steak-like, and when deglazed with a good port or herbed stock, delicious.

Diver's theory of cooking had become simpler, more provincial, over time. There had been mistakes. Smoked tofu frittata. The seitan experiments. And at the height of the fusion craze—the blood orange and scallion pizzette, which even in full public disclosure, Diver still felt was a legitimate dish, but ultimately was too foreign a taste for his guests. It never moved. And of course, therein lay one of Diver's many exasperations— people's fear of experimentation.

Life was exhausting. It had became more difficult to effectively argue against suicide, which was perhaps the reason religion outlawed it in the first place—fully aware of death's strange comforting grace, faith required some earnest moratorium against eating shotguns for breakfast. Moreover, the squalor of the world we created permeated a man's skin to the bone. It became impossible to wash off—and the flesh slowly sweated the ungodly suffering of millions drowning in our wake. Was this why Mary Magdalene washed the Christ's feet? Like art, which was a response to or a respite from the horror of the everyday, Diver's cooking forced the reaper to be patient, offering fruit in place of the fruitless, a repast for the famished. But what could one offer the waking dead? What could one offer those who, still breathing, did not live? Or who refused to taste?

Diver's greatest prejudice lied not in his disgust of ignorance, but in his hatred of those willfully so.

Diver was, when all said and done, keenly aware that he did not truly seek exile, or even exile lite, from the rest of the world. Rather what he sought was anonymity and solitude on his terms. He wanted acquaintances. He wanted to wave to people on the street who knew him and who would smile with appreciation as he walked by. But Diver also desperately wanted them to keep walking.

He wanted everyone at arms length—but kindly so. It seemed a simple request. He was happy to leave everyone else alone in return for the same.

His social contract was an obscure one, a misanthropic addendum to Locke. But it was not selfish. Nor was it conceded. It was simply, in his mind, recognition of his disposition—a knowing of himself he thought honest and uncomplicated. He wanted no responsibilities beyond his one sword thrust into the giant beast of suffering that haunted us all, too vast to be defeated by the futile pinpricks of individual combat.

Food was his connective tissue to society. It was how he interacted, and what he hoped would substitute for his presence.

After deftly chopping his morels, Diver placed several cloves of garlic on his cutting board and crushed them with the flat blade of his Hoffritz, smashing them to a pungent pulp. Adding this and the mushrooms to a glass bowl, he turned to dicing a large shallot with sea salt and fresh oregano. These ingredients he placed to the side of his range on a sheet pan and lit a flame under a thick-walled sauté pan. The pan grew hot as Diver added several ounces of virgin olive oil. As it began to release its fragrance and brown ever so slightly, Diver added four cups of fava beans he had boiled and drained earlier in the morning. They sizzled instantly. He remembered what his mentor, a Jordanian chef named Antoine, had taught him about pan searing. "You do not sauté with the hands," he said, "you sauté with the ears." Diver remembered not understanding at first. "Listen," Antoine said, having dropped several shrimp and scallops into his skillet. The little fellows squeaked and sizzled in butter. "Do you hear that?" he asked, "the sound of flavor. Now wait, do not touch them, do not move them, just listen…"

"It's getting louder," Diver responded.

"Yes," Antoine replied, "there is a moment when the pitch will be at its highest. When the natural sugars are caramelizing. That is the point of movement. That is the time to shake your pan, not before. Know this sound, and let it guide your hands. Do not rush. But do not be slow."

As the beans crescendoed, Diver deglazed them with brandy and added four cups of stock and escarole. He then added the morel mixture and turned down the heat. After a minute Diver transferred the food to a terracotta baking dish, topping the course with a dollop each of salted butter and caramelized beet puree. He then topped the dish with its lid and placed it into the oven at low heat.

Twenty minutes to perfection, Diver thought to himself, just before looking up to see Lanny enter the kitchen.

"Hi, Chef," he greeted Diver, as he did every day upon arriving at *De Terre*.

"Hey, Lanny. Doing well?"

"Not bad," he replied, "So, how are we looking tonight?"

"About twenty on the books," Diver replied, "Three four-tops, two deuces and a party of six at eight p.m. We'll be steady."

"New menu starts tonight?'

"Yeah. A few things. The soup is pumpkin bisque. The cassoulet has morel mushrooms, escarole and fava beans. I've changed the risotto. This month's has carrots, chard, and fontina cheese, finished with honey-roasted almonds. The honey is from Wyoming, all organic, from a Clearmont clover farm I know there. Really nice. I got some new wines in earlier as well. A few blushes from the Finger Lakes. Simon turned me on to them."

"You've been busy. The risotto sounds good. Do I remember...you did the chard thing last fall, too, yes?"

"Yeah, but with squash and pignolis. It was a good seller."

"I like chard. Why do I never buy it for myself?"

"The same reason I never do. It's work food."

"But I like your food," Lanny laughed. "I just can't replicate it."

"I have no skill that's not reproducible," John laughed. "I've got the bisque ready. Would you like to try some?"

"Yes, but let me get the bar ready first..." he trailed off. With that, Lanny passed through the door to the front of the house.

If Diver was truly a misanthrope he was certainly a unique one—he hadn't completely forsaken humanity but refused to be surprised by its shortcomings and depravity. Better stated, he *desired* to have faith, he *desired* to find something worth holding dear, but more typically swayed back and forth between sheer revulsion and mild disenchantment for his fellow man. Diver was a synthesis of many incomplete endeavors — a lapsed Buddhist, athlete, art historian, martial artist, transcendental meditator, poet, bodybuilder, musician, and son — but he was distinctly an Enlightenment thinker. A lover of quotation, he found himself quoting Kant more frequently than others, and no quote more closely matched his wishes than Kant's reference to sublimity as *a propensity to be moved...*

Diver had always found that statement beautifully poetic. The movement itself was a separate issue, but the *propensity* was what counted. For Kant, the desire for action seemed favored over action itself, allowing for potential to trump the kinetic. Texans had developed this little beauty into their common vernacular. They were always *fixin'* to do something, which did not necessarily mean ever doing it at all. Diver believed he had that propensity, and even in his lack of movement he remained open to moving. He just lacked direction.

Lanny offered hope to Diver, often on a daily basis, a slow rhythmic drip of hope. Not unlike the lotus, a symbolic beauty growing from ugliness, Lanny reminded Diver that real kindness frequently remained obscured by the vulgarity of common society.

Absent from the kitchen, Lanny strode into the front of the house, to the well-worn oak bar and began his prep work. While cutting lemon wedges, for perhaps the thousandth time of what might be a thousand more times, he glanced up at the north wall of the dining room. This was one of *De Terre's* most loved features, known affectionately as the "wall of truth" by its regulars. The wall itself was the only remaining surface bearing the signature of the building's first existence — that of a rope works. While Diver renovated the structure to reveal a cleaner, more modern shell, the wall of truth wall still bore the etched concrete patina that could only be the result of seventy-five years of life. That wall had witnessed the labor of hundreds of men, the trials of three American wars, the assassination of a president and, at least Diver was told, a death by stabbing.

Now, in *De Terre*, the wall had become interactive. The practice of inscribing it by patrons, born some time ago of the random intersection of a child and a crayon, had become tradition. Forsaking the occasional steel bolt, its great grey and black expanse was covered with a most refined graffiti — a plethora of quips, quotes, and questions in varied scale, color, and language.

Some of its selections included:
Indoor plumbing created Polio
Jackson Browne 6/30/07
If you ain't Dutch, you ain't much
And of course, there were the countless Bill loves Julies, the Pat + Crystal forevers, even a *Jane loves Jane* in green Sharpie. Birthdates, cartoon drawings, food reviews and trivia, often oriented towards American history, rounded out the other popular categories. And of languages, French, German, Italian and even Kiswahili were represented. Music enthusiasts would also note Levon Helm's signature over table number six. He had the snow pea fettuccini.

Together, the wall and its inscribers became a working definition of the philosophy of history. Text and structure merged both symbiotically and in contrary ways. Some scrawlings were propagandistic, serving the ego of its authors. Others were attempts at public assistance or education. Taken homogenously, it offered no context by which to be judged. One could not pinpoint its accuracy of the past any more than that of the future. It was warm but somehow impenetrable, despite its listing of wedding parties, concert venues and individual signatures. It could not be underestimated not could it be codified. It just became.

But Lanny, the wall of truth almost permanently etched in his visual memory, immediately noticed its newest new addition. The far left corner had a fresh entry. It must have been made the night before. The deuce at seven, Lanny presumed, an attractive couple. He had figured it was their forth or fifth date...there was intimacy but still some pretense. He was quiet. She was more jocular and smelled like patchouli. A bottle of pinot. Sweet pea lasagna. Seventy-three dollars with a fifteen-dollar tip. Twenty percent tippers were rare in those parts, and Lanny remembered them with the keenness of a detective. College students? No, he thought, too reserved. Post docs? Possible, but too relaxed. He fancied them to be adjuncts, recently hired instructors who connected at a lecture, a convocation perhaps. A little white wine at a reception turned into an exchange of business cards. A coffee soon after. And so the story begins.

As he walked closer to the wall Lanny read the new text. In chalk was written the equation *what is known $\leq$ what is believed.* Lanny grinned. Theirs was a fairly populist little town, a rare village in rural America where it was not unthinkable to see a local farmer having a casual conversation with a well-tattooed twenty-something filling his Vespa at a Hess station. It was more than likely that their fathers knew each other, or grandfathers, or that each had relatives in the local union, or VFW, or Elk's Lodge. The men on the local planning board were sons of the men on the last local planning board. There were fewer bookstores than silos. And far more pastures than parking lots.

This is not to describe a Utopia. Even with the university, there was a noticeable lack of color in the town. The majority population of Dutch and British families often murmured misgivings over Puerto Rican families moving into the area, as there was a general distrust of the large Hasidic community over the mountain.

There was, also, like so many working-class Northeastern towns, a tension that sat like spent groundwater beneath the crust of the place. A divide that included religion and race for sure, but more so, and perhaps most uniquely, a genuine hatred of a certain kind of change. At least this is how a newcomer might perceive it. Lanny, having been born there, understood the rift more precisely. There was, particularly amongst the town elders, a spiteful disdain towards the non-native developers and urbanites. It was a war that for some had been fought for generations — new zoning laws infringing on hunting grounds, unions succumbing to globalism, neighborhood associations eradicating backyard livestock — the slow unstoppable erosion of old country into the unsustainable new.

But this wasn't a town to take on Walmart. Rather, this was a town that Walmart would never notice. There was no theater. There was no shopping mall. There was simply not of a lot of profit to be made for a large enterprise. The local college was a highly ranked liberal arts enclave with a student body of around 2,300, giving the town half its population nine months a year. Carhartt and corduroy were neighbors in the department store. Like so many towns across the country, this was one that had no wherewithal to prepare for the future. It was attempting to find its way through the fog.

Lanny walked the dividing line of the town's philosophical gerrymander. As a native he could tell the difference between a Guernsey and a Holstein, but long ago, after graduating high school, he couldn't leave soon enough. Lanny was never deeply rooted. His family had moved four times before he was eighteen. At eighteen, he drove west until he hit the ocean and stopped. He had returned several years ago, a prodigal son of sorts, seeking a return to something meaningful, something reflective, something reborn.

Along the way he spent time in the desert. He befriended a few locals who drank heavily and shot speed between their toes. Their souls had been forfeited long ago. Unaware though they were; they glared open-eyed at the blazing sun like the gasping desiccated fish left homeless by the dying Salton Sea. One day after witnessing one of them beat his dog with a broom, Lanny took the poor creature into his truck and drove them both away to a new address.

In the mountains he found a job at a dinner theater. Lanny, his black lab, Harry, and a bellicose rooster who had adopted them both happily endured local productions of Rodgers and Hammerstein for a year or two. The pine trees were ageless beauties that rained on them their burnt sugar needles before turning to crushed straw. A forest fire put an end to most of them after a late summer drought. Harry died. Lanny kept going.

In the aftermath there was a commune, the death of a friend, a lover, a mild drug addiction, two bad novels, three wars, and a terrorist attack.

He headed east, through the desert again, now drier, angrier than before. The badlands. Small towns and their small town radio stations. Small churches. Suburban vacuity. Xenophobia. To the Midwest. Greasy diners. Light beer. Baseball hats and union signs. The Great Lakes and the abandoned factories of yesteryear. Buffalo, rising from the southward arc of Lake Erie along I-90 bore its bleached brick factories like the bandages of a wounded veteran. Turning south around the Finger Lakes to the trout kills, bejeweled with battered aluminum cans discarded after drinking parties. Home.

You could go home again, Lanny knew, but the trick was in waiting long enough to return. Now, moving back in middle age, Lanny renewed very few friendships from the past. It wasn't all by choice. Most were gone. Some were in Iraq or Afghanistan. Many had died. He saw their portraits in the paper.

It wasn't long after he returned that he saw the photo of Sergeant Levi Pence, heavy equipment technician, killed by an IED in Tikrit, along with three other men in his unit. Lanny knew the man, a classmate of his in high school, and son of one of his high school teachers.

When he attended the funeral service he saw Mr. Pence receive the flag from son's coffin folded crisply by the attendant soldiers in their military dress. They were expected to show no emotion, but be deeply reverent through their flawless regimented precision. They were older than Lanny expected, and several were women. Not a piece of their clothing hung loosely. Not a single hem was unpressed. As the coffin was lowered, a single bugler played taps. Mr. Pence shed single tears down each cheek in silence. There were only a handful of people in attendance. It was the most solemn event in which Lanny had ever participated.

At the end of the service Lanny approached Mr. Pence. He looked up from the ground and smiled when he saw Lanny.

"Why, Mr. Fontana," he said, "its lovely of you to come. Levi and I both always liked you."

"I'm sorry for your loss, Mr. Pence," Lanny responded, "Levi was a good man. And a patriot."

"And a good son, too. Please call me Simon."

"I wasn't sure you'd remember me," Lanny added.

"You don't live here anymore, do you, Lanny? Your parents moved to Florida, yes?"

"Yes," Lanny answered. "I'm back in town though. I've been here a few months. Getting my feet back under me..."

"Are you working?"

"Not yet. I'm looking."

"Good luck, my dear boy. I know it's hard. That's why so many are leaving this town. There's not much to keep them here I'm afraid. But it's nice to see you back again. And thank you so much for coming."

Lanny knew there wasn't much else to say. He knew Mr. Pence was alone, not unlike he was, but the difference in their situations was too great for the moment. Perhaps with time there'd be more to say...

As he left, he heard a young woman crying.

The soft twilight of early morning was Lanny's new comfort. He had forgotten silence when away. Awaking in the darkness — around 5 was best — he could sit in the obscurity and wait for the sounds of life to creep into his bedroom. First, the juncos, the mockingbirds. The roosters to follow, if they ever slept at all. The sound of the wind. A screen door squeaking. A dog barking. Then, out of his window he could see the farm lights slowly pulse. It was a time of great intimacy with the world. A time of great beauty — with precious few to crowd or destroy it. The drunks and the thieves were sleeping. Alarm clocks counted down, but the offices remained dark.

This perfect hour of night becoming day was Lanny's great solace. His mind was at its sharpest, his memories awaited perfect recall. The world around him exposed its nuances, its habits and its rhythms. Like an Arcadian checklist, its sequence quietly presented itself, and was soon interlaced with human activity. Methodically, the working class roused, invisible heroic bastards, making things run like the gods of the Iliad. Men whose days ended when most people broke for lunch. In the winter, they drove the plows. In the summer, the tractors. Garbage collectors. Newspaper carriers. Breakfast cooks.

Working moms. God bless them.

Then a splinter of sun over the cornfields. It's over. The magic ends. Day begins. You watch the news. You remember to hate your enemies. You curse an overdue bill. You pump gas into your car and spill jam on your pants. Soon thereafter, you find yourself in a restaurant slicing lemons as a respite from it all.

Four

My Trich is my own. Let me be with it...let me twist and pull my hair until it dies. As it does, it winds itself through my fingers and piles on my chair at the shoulder. I am shedding. I am losing myself. I am no bother to you. I am imperfect. I am flawed. I am not like others. This is my penance. Let me wrench. Let me heave. Let my fingers go numb. Let my arm tire. Let my scalp burn. Let me feel the pain at the base of my neck as I rip at my roots. Let my baldness define my compulsion. Look at me. Bear witness to my deficiency.

Diver looked down to see his cutting board littered with scraps of hair. He hadn't noticed removing his hat as his mind wandered.

He had once attended an Elie Wiesel lecture in college. The attendees were deeply reverent. The room was crowded. In it, a diverse audience parsed meaning—they were aware of their fortune, but were equally aware of the built-in inaccessibility of his experiences to them. Most were born twenty years after World War II. Most had never traveled outside of the country. Of those who had, few had been to Germany. Fewer still to Buchenwald.

What could it mean to travel to Buchenwald today? Its reality was subverted by the very existence of the choice to experience it in the first place. Buchenwald had offered no choice. Buchenwald had not seen its visitors leave, had not existed as a place to travel memories, or reflection. It stood in the contemporary era as a testament to atrocity, and as Adorno thought, an atrocity from which we forever forfeited our humanity.

After Auschwitz there can be no poetry.

Wiesel said many deeply moving things in his address. He wore his disgust for violence on his sleeve. He appealed to emotion, to decency. He refused to recognize the barbarity written into the code of human DNA. It was the single flaw in an otherwise flawless appeal — a noble one to be sure, but Diver thought a flaw nonetheless.

One thing Wiesel said permanently etched itself into Diver's memory. Wiesel stated that he had earned the right to turn his back on humanity, but that he had not. It was not the end of the statement that Diver thought compelling but the first — that one had to earn the right to forsake humanity. There was no opt-out button, it seemed, that was inherent upon birth. Unlike the modern idea of freedom, which included the freedom to not care, Wiesel argued for a freedom contingent upon participatory justice. Birthright required that one be one's brother's keeper.

As a homage, Diver grappled with the ramifications of Wiesel's statement every time he cut onions. He thought onions were as appropriate a trigger as anything — they were, he knew, the paid wages of Egyptian slaves under the Pharaoh Khufu — but he always remained aware of the absurdity of such a pairing. As such, he most often smiled uncomfortably with a Vidalia in his hand...it was his weight to bear.

With his hand, John brushed his hair into the trash and washed the cutting board. Back to task, he chopped away as the *De Terre* reading group conversed quietly in the dining room.

"Sometimes, I think our country might be near its end," Claire quietly and fatally sighed.

"What do you mean, Dear?" Simon answered.

"There's not much connecting us anymore. No one cares about their neighbors..."

"If we look at America as an organism," Bill added, "a living, breathing entity, from a biological perspective, it makes sense that it would be mortal. If a nation is a collective of human life, wouldn't a nation die just as people die?"

That Saturday they were reviewing Alexis de Tocqueville. Diver, fresh from his onioned malaise, soon brought a platter of food to their table. A bottle of unfiltered Spanish wine in a decanter was already half drunk.

Simon answered Bill. "But society is not an organism. It is a social contract based largely on fear and protection. You are comparing apples to oranges." He paused with his hand on his chin. "But even if I grant your analogy, America need not share our biology."

When Diver entered from the kitchen, Claire had drifted from the conversation. She found herself attracted to him, even as quiet and sullen as he was. There was something about John that she wanted to know more about, but she would have to defy her shyness to succeed. The truth was, she was more interested in him than in Tocqueville.

"These look lovely, John," Claire interjected, looking up at Diver. "What are we eating?"

"Fried pierogies," John answered proudly, "stuffed with caramelized onions, deglazed brandy and red potatoes. With that some roasted corn and peach salsa. Vitosky's crop — right up the road."

"Join us, John," Simon offered. "I've brought some wine from my trip to the lake."

"Well," John surmised, "I'll have a glass, but then back to the kitchen. I'm on the clock...got some saffron to bleed."

"How violent," Bill laughed, "for a vegetarian."

"Everything bleeds," John answered, pouring himself a glass of cabernet.

"Which leads us back to our topic," replied Bill. "Claire is worried that America is dying."

"Just as a concept," Claire reiterated.

"What was it Tocqueville said?" John offered, "That when push comes to shove Americans will choose equality over freedom?"

"Almost exactly" Simon answered.

"What do you think, John?" Claire asked, slowly testing her wine's legs.

"Our experiment might be over sooner than later." John shrugged. "Most people forget Greece only lasted about 400 years. That's not much compared to Egypt or Byzantium. Of course, Greece left it all on the field, so to speak. Live fast, die young. The Janis Joplin of nations. When we do go out, we'll leave quite an historical postscript, both good and bad."

"The Janis Joplin of nations..." Claire reflected.

Simon winced. "No. No. No. She was too unkempt. And a bit tawdry don't you think? How about the Thurman Munson of nations?" he asked, "I like that one much better."

"Thurman Munson it is," John agreed. "To legacies." John raised his glass to toast.

The group toasted to heroes lost. "To Thurman," they said in unison.

"So the question might then be," John continued, "following Claire's worry, if America is dying, what is killing her? Tocqueville, if I remember correctly, criticizes the tyranny of the majority, which of course, will define freedom according to its terms. Now, true freedom scares the hell out of most people. What people really want is to feel safe, even at the cost of freedom, which goes back to Simon's comment about the social contract."

"I'm more worried about the tyranny of the minority these days," Jacob interjected. "Millionaires and the religious right are exerting more influence on politics than their numbers should dictate. And they only believe in their definitions of freedom.

"The beating heart of America is capitalism. And capitalism may be unsustainable. It encourages acquisition. Acquisition requires protection. Protection constricts freedom."

"We're discussing this on too theoretic of a level," Claire said. "I'm talking about something else. Something more day to day. It might be anecdotal but it seems very real. We have become divided. We have become mean. Risking little ourselves, we love to see other people fail. Sex scandals. Car chases. Reality TV. Celebrity divorce. Hate radio. I can't even watch the news anymore. It's all partisan. No one wants to see someone they disagree with succeed even in the slightest way. We love to drag people down."

John continued. "Walter Benjamin said that there is no document of civilization that is not at the same a document of barbarism. People don't seem to learn much from history. Maybe admitting that we are not so exceptional would be a great start."

Simon thereafter brought his glass to his lips, swallowing its large last gulp of wine. "Freedom is just too difficult for most people," he abruptly stated, rising and walking away to the bathroom, "just as being an American is."

As Simon walked to the bathroom, the reading group exchanged curious glances, looking slightly shocked.

"We'll just have to continue that..." Bill noted.

"But without me," John offered. "I have to go."

"Such a shame," Claire said with a sigh, "you always leave when things get interesting, John. Stay for a bit."

Bill answered her. "John is the last of the stoics, Claire. He prefers solitude to company. And, for that matter, dislikes most things as far as I can tell — except good food and spirits."

"I tolerate you, don't I?" John quipped back.

"Touché." Bill responded.

Claire was intrigued. "Defend yourself, Chef. Are you truly a denier of pleasure?"

John noticed her smiling at him. For a moment, he felt like they were alone. "I wouldn't put it that way. Perhaps I just find pleasure in things others typically don't."

"Like what?" she continued, not missing a beat.

John responded with a wry smile, "Thornton Wilder put it best I think: solitude without loneliness."

"You always quote other people. What do you do when you're alone? Do you like music?"

John shook his head. "Music is a waste of silence."

"Movies?"

"Sometimes. I like Japanese Samurai movies. I also follow sports, hockey mostly."

"Strange, I would never have guessed that."

"After we just shared a Yankee moment? I've been a fan since I was young. It kind of began with my father."

Claire was curious. "Really? How?"

"Well, my parents were poor. I grew up poor. My dad was a former Triple-A pitcher on the Phillies farm team. He taught me that sports were the last level playing field. It didn't matter what color your skin was. Or who your parents were. Or where you lived. Or how much money you had. If you practiced harder than the guy next to you, you started. And if you played better than the guy opposing you, you won. And no one could take that from you."

"That's a nice story," she continued.

"Not altogether. I found out he was wrong. The system was rigged. Just like everything." His eyes fell.

"A toast to equality!" Bill laughed.

"What about the Japanese thing?" Claire prodded.

"Just the classics. *The Sword of Doom* is my favorite."

"What's the draw?" Claire asked.

"The ethics," John answered. "Now I leave you to your book."

Claire looked to persuade John to stay, but Bill spoke first.

"Let the man go, Claire," Bill interrupted. "Save your inquisition for Simon, who left us with that juicy bombshell before his bladder failed him."

Claire sighed in a moment of frustration, but conceded. "OK then. Last question, John. What scares you? What keeps Chef Diver up at night?"

John looked down at Claire. "Wow. Um. Quite the question," He tried his best to seem unfazed. "Where did that come from?"

Claire teased, "You tell me yours and I'll tell you mine." She smiled in an attempt to sit him back down.

John beat back his nervousness. He was uncomfortable, but offered a forthright answer. "Failure," he responded.

"What, with your restaurant?" she asked.

"No, at life," John stated flatly, and then winked at Claire genially before walking away from the table. He did not turn around. As he pushed his way through the double doors to the kitchen, he passed Simon returning from the back of the house.

While recalculating his culinary chores, John first checked the mung beans happily stewing in their steam kettle, dropping some dried spice into the mixture. He then slowly ran a thumb over his Hoffritz, encompassed again by the dull hum of his overhead exhaust fan. Time to wash the filters. He could tell by the sound. It was a job he detested, but completed rather faithfully every six weeks. But not right now. His blade needed a quick honing before beginning its next task — slicing thin threads of fresh basil, followed by poached white asparagus minced with chives and sea salt. Diver was making soufflés for the weekend's special. Wonderfully rich yet light pillows of cheese, savory herbed custard and whipped egg whites swollen with air and baked into a buttery golden dome. As Diver deftly cut the asparagus with great precision, then minced it finely with salt to enhance its flavor and texture, he pondered the delicacy, like he did sports, as a metaphor for the human situation. There's a time limit, he thought, you have more time to prepare than execute...no second chances, no going back. Soufflés were like life, he pondered with a smile, you either rise or you fall. As he began to shred some Taleggio, he could still hear the cacophony of the reading group in the dining room.

Five

"So you think you've got me pegged, " Simon directed to Bill, "You think you have me all figured out, huh? Well, let me tell you what I believe, and what I stand for." Simon poured a long glass of Spanish wine and paused to swallow a deep drink from his stemless glass.

"I'm a Buckley conservative. The last of a dying breed. Do not confuse me with a Republican. I believe in the frugality of government — and that 50 percent plus one does not mean justice. I believe Madison was right. He worried about placing too much power in the hands of the unwashed masses. And I'm not talking about cleanliness. I'm talking about laziness, about willful ignorance — the insipid celebration of dumb that defines our culture. The sheep. Sheep shouldn't get to vote.

"People forget America is an experiment," he continued, "on more than one level. First, it requires an educated electorate. We are called to watch the watchmen. Patriotism is hard, its active, its uncomfortable. It means you fight for the right of an idiot to burn the flag. Even if it makes you sick. You fight for the right of a teenager to pierce his nose, or wear his pants below his ass. It means you compromise. You leave people alone so they will in turn leave you alone. And when you have to see each other, you wave politely and say thank god we are all Americans, even if you hate them. And hating them as you do, if their house is on fire you grab some water and help put it out.

"America doesn't exist as a canvas on which to paint your religion. Or your right-to-life badge. Or your fear of change. Or your dreams of yore. It exists as a contract — as strong only as the courage of the men and women who fight to protect it and who hold it dear. Men like my son." Simon paused for another sip of his wine and then continued. "The American contract creates those most unnatural of things — things like desegregated neighborhoods, moderate laws, upward mobility, a blind court of justice, a strong middle class — and proclaims, like god on the seventh day, that they are good.

"But this contract is made frail is its tenuous marriage to capitalism. Capitalism is, as John said, completely amoral. It must be regulated ethically, with respect to real human concern. Sure, I believe in the free market, but I am not stupid, nor am I disingenuous. You can't play a fair game on a tilted field. We could all use another Teddy Roosevelt.

"But don't misunderstand me. You do not get to have what I have. It's not a question of the ends. It's a question of means. It's a question of what is earned. What you get are the same chances I get, the same possibilities, the same access. And that's where we part. And we compete. That's where we claim our independence by utilizing the gifts given to us by our maker in the free marketplace, to claim the American dream.

"Which leads me back to my original point," Simon said while gesturing wildly. "Freedom. The unfettered ability to follow your dream. To invent a product. To compose your aria. To make your mark. With it you win big or fail spectacularly — but it's all you. Freedom is like a ropewalk without a net. It is the greatest gift this country offers and it the one cherished the least. Why? The answer goes back to the sheep. Sheep fear freedom. They want a dog to guide them home. They want a fence with strong posts. They want a scapegoat to blame for their own shortcomings — whether it's immigrants, or communists, or zealots, or liberals, or the green party or K Street. They want permission to hate someone other than themselves. And their flocks are growing. We may have been exceptional once, but I think we are exceptional no more."

With that, Simon exhaled deeply and looked out the window of the restaurant. Storm clouds hung in the east. A tow truck drove down the road. He could tell it was cold outside by the clarity of the glass.

"What you have," he finished, "like Rousseau feared, is a country where theater has replaced reality. We are rehearsing from a misinterpreted script."

When Simon stopped speaking the group was silent for a moment. Bill was the first to respond.

"Wow, Simon," he sighed, "that's about the most I can remember you've ever said at once." He paused. "So…what's your answer?"

"Answer?" Simon laughed.

"Yeah. Answer. What's the answer to the problem? The sheep. The fear of freedom. The whole Rousseau thing."

Claire shifted in her chair. "Sheep aren't really afraid of freedom, guys," she interjected, "There's a problem with your metaphor. In fact, I think I read that sheep are quite smart."

"It's true. You're correct, Claire," Simon answered, "Sheep are most likely not afraid of freedom. What I do know, however, is that sheep follow other sheep. They are herd animals. In this sense they are like humans. And in this sense humans are like sheep."

"That may be," Claire replied. "People do like to fall in line."

"And politicians like making lines for people to follow," Bill interjected. "Our sheep analogy notwithstanding, we have yet to define the cure for our problem. What are we to do, Simon?"

"The solution seems too complex," Simon answered. "It requires a complete re-write of our popular culture, no? Any remedy would find itself struggling to swim upstream in the river of crap our media serves up."

"For someone with Plato issues, Simon," Bill quipped, "you sound an awful lot like Socrates."

Simon smiled. "Maybe I do. Maybe I do. I spent seventeen years trying to teach young men and women to think for themselves. To think critically. You might say I was teaching geography. You'd be right of course. But more than anything I was trying to get them to unlearn what they already believed — that school is too hard or too stupid to care about. Or that nothing really mattered anyway. Most of them couldn't even find Israel on a map. Couldn't find Minnesota for that matter. But that's another problem. The dumbing down of America. Or maybe it's a part of the same problem. I guess it's not my worry now. I'm retired. I'm at the end of my usefulness. Maybe I wasn't that useful to begin with."

He finished the last sip of his wine and stood up. "Anyway, I'm tired of talking," said Simon. "I'm going to head on home."

With that Simon exchanged goodbyes and left *De Terre*. As he closed the door behind him, he could just hear Diver chopping away in the kitchen. Bill and Claire remained seated and continued to drink at the table.

"You know," Claire said to Bill, "John never asked me what my greatest fear was."

"I imagine telling me is not the same as telling him," Bill responded.

"You're a smart cookie, Bill" she smiled, then rose to leave, a bit wobbly from too much afternoon wine.

Six

There are certain nights that the world seems just about perfect, whether the result of the sun tipping into the west with vivid color, the briskness of the evening air, the cooing of ring-necked doves on warm roof shingles, or the comforting blackness that disappears the hostility of the day. On special nights all those things happen together, making for the most perfect moments. And as Klara Dankowski looked down at her newly born daughter, she thought that all those most perfect things compared unfavorably to her daughter's eyes. The bleating little red-haired child that looked up at her was the last greatest thing ever made. And she was lucky enough to be the woman who brought it to the world.

She died having never doubted that belief.

Claire knew her mother only in memories. "I named you after me," she would say. "Your father wanted to name you Lucy, after his favorite actress. But she's too silly."

Those memories were good ones. Her parents owned a laundromat in a small Berkshire town. Claire would work there every summer, doing the fluff and fold six days a week, which gave her mom extended time to visit her sisters in Somerville.

Her father's name was Teodor, but everyone knew him as Ted. He was a jovial man prone to emotions. He cried during romantic movies, and wept after the death of their family hamster, Spaetzle. He would tell Claire a joke of the day every morning. He would have looked them up the night before. First, in his joke books, later, on the internet. In fact, Claire was convinced that her father thought the internet was little more than a giant joke encyclopedia.

"Why aren't bananas ever lonely?

"Why, Daddy?"

"Because the come in bunches!"

Claire's mother would cook for thirty people. Her pots and pans were so large they often spanned two burners on the stovetop, which was advantageous for quicker heating. Gallons of cream soups, voluminous casseroles and ever-present macaroni salads crowded the icebox and the chest freezer in the basement.

"If you are going to cook, cook once for ten days," she would say.

From an early age, Claire loved to read. She read the Hardy Boys. *The Island of the Blue Dolphins*. Nancy Drew. Judy Blume. C.S. Lewis. As she entered middle school she was placed ahead a grade, and moved from 5th to 7th with the blessing of her parents, who were very proud of her grades. Each of them had never gone beyond high school, but were successful businessowners. They worked hard, and were financially comfortable even if they lived frugally. They impressed in Claire the importance of an education. They helped her with homework. They took her to church. They enrolled her in ballet.

Claire was thirteen when her mother became ill. It was June, and cooler than usual in that time of year. The wind came off the mountains at night. Klara grew fatigued beyond her years, no longer cooking great masses of foods in the kitchen. Her breathing became labored, just enough so that one could notice if one listened closely.

Claire listened closely.

Claire would go open the laundromat herself on the days her father took her mother to the doctor. Their neighbor Alvin would check in on Claire and sit reading magazines. They would go to the doctor several times a week, many times to a new doctor. Across town. Across the state. It would be July when Claire first heard the word cancer.

And in December of that same year, she watched a Roman Catholic priest offer words meant to comfort them. His aged face was wrinkled deeply, slightly obscured by the black-rimmed glasses that covered his brown eyes. Claire remembered wondering if he believed in angels like her mother did, and if so, if he'd seen the ones her mother talked to. As she watched her father's tears fall in waves down his face, as she hugged him with all her strength, and wished it was all a joke — an elaborate prank played by her father that he read about online — Claire knew she would never be the same.

Her mother was buried on the coldest day of the year.

In her senior year of high school, Claire received a full college scholarship. For several years she had poured herself into her studies. Making friends was not difficult for her, but it did not consume her the way that it did her peers. Boys were attracted to her. She dated occasionally. She went sleigh riding in the winter.

In the summers she continued to work in the laundromat with her father. It was more than a full year after her mother's death that she remembered him telling her a joke again. It was a joke he used to tell her long ago.

"What's brown and sticky?"

"What, Daddy?"

"A stick!"

As much as Claire had changed in those last several years her father had changed more. He put up a brave face for his daughter, but she knew he was not a tough man. And she loved that about him. She heard him cry at night in his bed. He would wake with eyes reddened from lack of sleep. But he loved his daughter, and even gained strength from her, knowing Klara would want them to stay strong together, to succeed, to grow, to laugh again.

So it was Claire who cooked huge pots of food for both of them. It was Claire who cleaned his favorite sofa seat, and filled the freezer with casseroles. And it was Ted who paid their bills, and enrolled her in ballet classes. It was Ted who bought Claire's first corsage, and who helped her with her homework. And it was Claire who loved him dearly.

There was a part of Claire that knew it was her role to have a child someday. To give her father a granddaughter that would fill him with life again. Her mother would tell her *a family is the most important thing*. At the time, she did not take it seriously. And while there was much to accomplish before she started one of her own, Claire understood what her mother had meant.

On the day of her commencement ceremony, Claire stood on stage for a moment her father would never forget. Her thick red hair was cropped short over her eyes, which held the kind of beauty that only strong men could find. She was confident but vulnerable, still keeping her trauma. As she reached out to receive her diploma, her father snapped a picture that he would later put in a scrapbook he kept for Klara.

After the ceremony, they went to the nicest restaurant in town. Claire's father had made a reservation one month before. He ordered a bottle of red wine that he let Claire sip when the waiter turned his head. His tongue loosened from the spirits, and he talked more freely than Claire ever remembered him doing before.

"Tonight, my little girl has become an independent woman," he said, toasting in the air. "I'm so proud of you, my sweetheart."

"Thank you, Daddy," Claire replied, seeing his eyes moisten.

"I want you to go and live your life," he said. "No worrying about me."

"I'll be just three hours away, Dad," Claire pleaded.

"That's not what I mean," he responded, taking Claire's hand in his. "I don't want you to fritter away opportunities. Your mother's passing forced you to grow up too early. Sometimes I worry that you're too serious. But how could you not be? You had to take care of me when I should have taken care of you."

"That's not true," Claire said, pressing his hand.

"I want to tell you something and I want you to promise me you'll never forget."

"Of course, Daddy."

He took a rectangular jewelry case from his jacket. He opened it to reveal a gold necklace. "This belonged to your mother. Your grandmother gave it to her. Your mother never wore it. She was always afraid it would fall off, because the clasp was a bit weak. But I had the clasp repaired. Before she died, your mother told me to give this to you on your graduation day. She wanted you to think of a celebration when you wore it."

He offered it to Claire who took it with a deep breath. The eighteen-carat chain was simple but elegantly woven with individually hammered links. As she put it on she felt it ride high on her neck, like a choker.

"That looks beautiful," her father said.

"I'll never take it off," Claire answered.

Ted grasped his daughter's hand once more. "Claire," he said, leaning into her, "promise me you'll never forget." He took a long breath and checked himself against the water welling in his eyes. "If you ever see something in this world you want, go get it. Don't waste time. Time has a way of taking things away from you."

Seven

Tears are the first confirmation of a good onion. Diver blinked repeatedly from the wonderful fumes which, while acrid, foretold of a well-rounded gravy for that evening's special. He used the term gravy in the Italian sense—describing his rich tomato sauce heavy with garlic and fresh peas. Sauce went under things, not on top. And as the thick tomato paste bubbled over a low fire on the range, Diver wafted the aroma of the mixture to his nose with his right hand. He could tell it needed another Vidalia. The sweetest and most robust of bulbs, they were a local mainstay—pulled from the black dirt not 30 miles from *De Terre*.

Diver's Akwesasne grandmother had pulled such bulbs for most of her life, knees bent on the soft ground, hands leathered from the dry thinly bladed greens. He remembered her sun darkened face and white hair—a woman of great strength—who could pull a roasting pan from the oven with her bare hands. She was stern but not cruel, revealing little emotion outside of a familiar scalding anger. Every winter she made Christmas dinner for twenty in a kitchen no more than several paces long. One range and four burners. And even from the confines of the diminutive children's table tucked into the

corner — that somehow magically sat him and his five cousins —
Diver saw her command of every square inch of that space. He
marveled at her control of each utensil. The whisk. The slotted
spoon. The hand-cranked food mill. It was she who commanded
his attention, not the *Godzilla* movies, not the gifts of socks and
underwear, not the sips of beer his grandfather gave him for
fetching new bottles. She was the master of that kitchen, and as a
result, the master of that house.

　　Diver thought of her more often in the winter, when the
black dirt lay dormant, and the winds brought in the first wet
pangs of cold across the face. But after the diced Vidalia
squeaked in his olive-oiled skillet and slowly dissolved to form a
glassy savory reduction, his thoughts turned to Claire, which he
thought odd, and her earlier fear of a dying America.

　　He wanted to tell her that it did not matter. That America
was never fully born in the first place — at least in accord with its
noble ideals. And that if it were to die, or if it had died already,
that we would be the last to know. That there were men — men
who lived in shadows, who were groomed from birth in secreted
circles, who were the sons of supremacy, children of
commanders, who lived lives ordained to determine life and
death like small gods, men who prayed to Machiavelli and
Churchill, who married only to bear the son who would replace
him, men for whom force was a signature, sacrifice was isolation,
and valor was a fiction — these were the men who governed
America's dying. And it was not the calling of a reading group to
ask such questions.

　　He wanted to tell her that it did not matter. That America
would only be a paragraph in the monograph of history. Like all
countries. Like all kingdoms. Like all principates. That time
erased all traces of human momentum. As if it were competitive.
As if it could be. One of four dimensions pressing violently like a
vice squeezing the swollen melon of human existence into pulp.
Pulp that dries into humus. And humus that dries into sand.
And sand that blows into dust. So is the fate of men. So is the fate
of borders men cross. So is the fate of lines men draw.

And he wanted to tell her that it did not matter. That Montaigne was right. That ignorance is the softest pillow on which we rest our heads. And that we love our comfort so.

He wanted to tell her that it did not matter. Because evil was banal. And that no one had the time to really care anymore anyway. They were too busy watching TV.

He wanted to tell her that it didn't matter. That the onions needed his attention. And that at the end of the day, a good gravy was the only problem really able to be solved.

And he wanted to tell her that it mattered more than anything.

Was it possible, John questioned, to spend one's life in a constant search for something deeply meaningful while being simultaneously too exhausted to find it?

The answer was elusive.

The onions kept bubbling.

And who was tasked with the search? Who was one to question anything?

One had to start in the past…it could begin with Locke, at least to make things simpler. In the state of nature man was vulnerable, unhappy, constantly living in fear and subject to nature's greatest law. Survival of the fittest. Only the strongest survive. In a state of nature man was prey to the will of the stronger. And so began the social contract. In this contract we divided labors, we built communities with walls, we farmed, we clothed, we all contributed in specialized ways to advance community. And for this we are protected by a common defense. We are safer together than we are alone. In this contract even artists and poets have a role—the role of reinforcing the community. And enter paintings of the royal class, paintings of Christ, sculptures of the Buddha, history paintings, and monuments to war.

In the west, these roles were codified in the classical era and again solidified in the Renaissance within a sanctioned standard of quality and beauty…realism was king, and artists' skills were measured by their ability to capture reality in the most lifelike fashion. So stone becomes flesh and you move from

Michelangelo to Bernini to Rodin in a seamless progression of excellence.

And this pattern continues for two thousand years or so. Forward to the last decade of the nineteenth century and the Impressionists blow it all up. They subvert the canon of realism and project their imaginations upon the world. Art becomes the residue of the mind, and creativity is aligned with a unique vision of the singular artist's pursuit. Gauguin, Van Gogh, Duchamp, Picasso. They break the rules. And with the rules broken there is only one place for artists to go, and that's inward. Realism has been dethroned.

Modernists run with this idea. They deny even the slightest nod to any aspect of the real world. Interiority becomes the path to truth. They attempt a universal language based on nonobjective abstraction. The cube. The zip. The line. You get Rothko, Newman, Kline, Brancusi, Calder. Everything becomes reductive. Everything becomes minimal.

But this very movement, as significant as it is artistically, moves art increasingly away from the day-to-day life of the larger community. It is now the personal expression of an individual, and not the veneration of a shared culture or way of life.

As problematic as this is for the artist's relationship with the public, it also undermines the artist's relationship to quality. How does one critique a product of the mind without reference to the real world? How does one judge a good color from a bad color? A good cube from a bad cube? What is our place in the world if we cannot know for what it is we stand?

And how can we know where we stand if we do not know where we once stood?

No artists, no poets, no philosophers, no politicians, no generals, no priests, no judges are left to help us. We have lost the standards by which to measure.

John ended his thought suddenly, and brought another beer to his lips, downing its last few ounces. He bit the inside of his mouth.

He sighed and laughed at himself, shaking his head. He stirred his gravy.

He decided not to tell Claire anything.

Eight

When finally the sides of the mouth are too raw, the incisors are prefect for picking the flesh of the front. Gently first, like a tease, and then more daringly, pinch the tissue between the top and bottom teeth and pull it away. The pain pierces through the cheeks and shoots behind the eyes. This could go on for hours if patient enough. Each action making a more precise sting, each sting a more loving embrace. There could be nothing more wholly deserved than this time with yourself. With every weeping pore you attest to your life. And to your life you offer this sacrifice of flesh. With luck there will be sores to pop in the morning that trickle down the throat.

With butter browning, squeaking, bubbling, in his cast-iron skillet, Diver added celery and diced red pepper, a clove of garlic, and whole black peppercorns. They sizzled together and caramelized quickly. After deglazing with a mix of fresh tomato puree and Champagne, he removed the skillet from the heat and set the pan aside.

His lower lip was now inflamed. Worse than before. Diver, like many people, burdened himself with self-doubt and a lack of confidence. During particularly difficult times, he hated himself for the savageness of his species, mortal sins that he bore as a member of the tribe. Frequently, he attempted to reassure himself, however tenuously, that being conscious of the hypocrisy and evil of humankind was enough to elevate him from the masses.

We are all guilty in everything before everyone.

As an illusion, it was enough to keep him going...enough to keep from using his Hoffritz for more than cutting vegetables.

During better times he attempted to contribute to some kind of legacy that might be redemptive, that might help mitigate the shit that covered the Earth as a result of human waste. Of course the irony was not lost on him that his profession helped contribute to another kind of waste altogether.

As Diver turned back to his cutting board Lanny entered the kitchen, as he always did, perfectly on time and perfectly pleasant.

"Hi, Chef."

Diver looked up. "Hey, Lanny. How's the world today?" He felt his words mumbled.

"Pathetic," he replied. "Though I remain defiantly cheerful."

"You're my rock, Lanny. I don't know what I'd do without you." Diver knew this clichéd but true. He looked up at the clock. "Have you heard anything from the bank yet?"

"Not yet...should be any day though. I hope."

Lanny was trying to open his own business. For the past year he had saved, planned, plotted, and strategized with Diver. His idea was a simple one: to open a school that offered fun and simple hands-on cooking classes for parents and children. After countless hours of brainstorming, Lanny christened it "The Family Kitchen." It would offer weekend and after-school budget-friendly classes in a buoyant atmosphere. A sample schedule might include lasagna 101, homemade cheese, advanced meatball strategies and chocolatology. It revolved around a simple premise — that cooking offered a means for parents and children to spend time together. That the kitchen was the social center of the home. And that a family dinner, the part of the day increasingly becoming extinct, was ripe for a comeback.

But for all of Lanny's planning, he could not have predicted the recession. And in a time when credit became more desperately needed it became cruelly limited. Banks had made billions in an unregulated fiscal orgy. After pocketing their cache amidst the crash they helped cause, it was soon time to punish the populace for its subsequent accusations of corruption, for its daring fantasy of middle-class security, and also, as it had been whispered secretly, just for fun. They had all the power, and they were enjoying running the game.

But to a businessman, the game also created opportunities. Chief among them was the vast number of recently available properties. Companies were relocating, consolidation, merging, and bankrupting their way into the new American century. Home Depots were killing the hardware stores. Olive Gardens were killing the diners. Amazon was killing the bookstores. In the face of such a lopsided battle, Lanny donned a helmet to join the fight. When the internet cafe and vegan snack bar on Blair Street (corner lot with ample parking) shut its doors—its brightly painted red double doors that faced across the street to a dog park and community garden—Lanny knew the time had finally come to put his dream to action. He had found the last part of his puzzle—the perfect location.

When Lanny sat down with the loan officer from the local branch he had banked with for more than seven years, he did so as a stranger. Small banks no longer seemed to take the time to know their clients either by face or by name, and his was no exception. He shook hands politely with a man who introduced himself as Mark Stofner, and proceeded to tell him the story of The Family Kitchen. He listed his objectives, his mission statement, his business plan, his relevant experience. After much nodding, Mark pulled Lanny's financials, indicated that he was familiar with the address of the internet cafe, and that it was a property owned by an investment firm with which they made many transactions. Lanny was asking for a startup loan and line of credit for equipment purchases totaling seventy-five thousand dollars. After an hour of completing paperwork, Mark invited Lanny to return the following week.

Lanny left the office feeling optimistic. His financial plan seemed solid. The property required a monthly lease of two thousand three hundred dollars. He approximated utilities at six hundred dollars monthly. Insurance and liability were another seven hundred. One or two employees at nine to twelve dollars an hour. A loan payment of twelve hundred per month. It came out to roughly five grand of monthly overhead, including food. Based on this figure, he proceeded to cost out his classes. If a two-hour class were priced at seventy-five dollars (including free recipe and kid's apron), he would need to make two hundred fifty dollars a day (the kitchen would be closed Mondays and Tuesdays) to cover his expenses. This roughly equated to 70 customers per month. It seemed very doable.

The following week Lanny returned to the bank to be greeted by Mark, a man Lanny found sincere and honest even in their brief encounter. Mark invited Lanny to his cubicle where he sighed faintly and removed his glasses.

"We have just a few problems," he began softly.

"What are they?" Lanny returned.

"For one, your FICO score. It's certainly not bad, but it's a bit low for your requested loan. That, combined with your few assets means you're going to need some help."

"What kind of help?"

"A guarantor. Someone local with a successful business history would be helpful, but even then we have a problem with your lack of collateral, Lanny. You rent and are still financing your car with us. What you really need is a pledged asset."

"My car payments are only for five more months," Lanny interrupted, "then I'm free and clear."

"I see that, Lanny, but I'm only allowed to process this application based on the information I have at its date of submission."

"Are there better options?"

"The better option is a business partner. As a co-venture, I see this as being much more viable."

"But this is my dream, Mark. It's my vision."

"OK, Lanny. I understand," said Mark. He paused and rubbed his forehead with two fingers. "So you need a financial backer. Someone willing to invest in your kitchen. We probably couldn't agree to your total request, but there's a greater chance we could make something happen with more security. When we have pledged cash assets, we can usually make a loan for double the deposit. I can stretch that a bit for you, I think, with the blessing of the committee."

"What are we talking about?" asked Lanny as he took out a notepad and prepared to write.

"If you could obtain an investor willing to make a substantial deposit into an account with us we could probably extend a business line of credit to you of fifty thousand dollars somewhere at a revolving APR between eight and twelve percent, based on market conditions. We can set up a CD that covers our collateral concerns and even makes you some interest in the long run."

"What's substantial?" Lanny queried. He was jotting as he spoke.

"Twenty thousand," Mark replied, "plus the seven you have in your savings."

"That puts me all in," Lanny answered.

"And we'd be all in with you."

It was days after that conversation, days Lanny spent in a restless knot of anxiety, that he first realized Diver would be his only hope. His family, at least those he held dear, were no better off than he. His father, a union member all his life, had retired on a pension two years ago. His mother still worked occasionally as a freelance writer for a local farm bulletin. His brother, with whom he rarely spoke, sold Toyotas three states away.

Lanny found himself in the unenviable position of needing someone's help. It was hard enough to ask, but harder still to *have* to ask.

"Don't worry, Lanny, you'll know soon. And when they call, it will be good news." John offered. "I'm more worried about replacing you than I am about anything else. What am I going to do without you?"

"That's easy. Hire a cute young college girl and double your business," Lanny laughed back. "I don't exactly bring in the 'it' crowd, John."

"Have you seen my regulars? I swear Bill's beard alone is going to shut me down for health violations."

"He's here practically every week. And you know he loves you, John."

"And he is loved back, as are all of my hungry misfits. They are my people. And they will miss you as much as I will."

"Oh, please," Lanny said with a smile. "Not by half as much, if at all. Tell me, what's on tap tonight?"

Diver was happy to turn the subject to food, even though he knew he would soon miss such conversations. "The pasta tonight is penne with fresh peas, cherry tomatoes and a tarragon reduction. That will go really nice with the wine we got in last week. Also I've got wheat crust pizza with asparagus, portabellas, cotija and topped with fresh arugula. The quiche tonight is fried eggplant with chevre and the soup is a leek tomato, which is very light, and I'm serving that with a sliced boiled egg and cracked pepper.

"Got it. Are we still out of the soufflé?"

"Until tomorrow. I'm waiting on the truffles."

With that, Lanny pushed himself out of the swinging doors separating the kitchen from the front of the house. Once in the dining room, he began to place fresh candles and clean flatware on the tables. He took special care to ensure the six-top was level, as it had lost one of the swivels at its base the night before. A small piece of wood now took its place, hidden beneath a white tablecloth, which, like all *De Terre's* tables, was well made and neatly pressed.

He turned on the stereo behind the bar to hear the last segment of *Prairie Home Companion*, still airing in the face of obscurity. He checked the reservation book. Most people knew to call ahead for large tables in the small dining room. Tonight there was nothing but a few deuces and four tops, and Lanny knew several of them by name.

He returned to the kitchen and entered its sizable walk-in. Diver did not like freezing things. He put a premium on fresh ingredients, which is why the walk-in was larger than one would expect for a restaurant that size. Lanny knew this. He had come to know many things about Diver, despite his solitude, his introversion. He grabbed a handful of lemons and limes from their crates, a stalk of celery and a blood orange. He checked for other needs quickly before exiting and turning to Diver on the line.

"Guess who's coming to dinner?"

Diver looked over from his steam trays. "Who?"

"Claire and a friend. That's twice this week, John."

"She likes my food."

Lanny looked wryly at John. "She likes you, John. She likes *you*."

"No, she has more sense than that."

"You can't be this blind. She always asks for you when she's here."

Diver began to turn potatoes with a small paring knife. "Do you need an apron?" he said, ignoring the subject at hand.

"I've got one," Lanny replied, turning back to the dining room, "and you know I'm right. Instead of hiding, you should be dancing in the streets. She's gorgeous, you know."

A classically turned potato should have seven sides. This was one of many arcane rigors of culinary excellence that Diver greatly loved and appreciated. Gourmet cuisine demanded the same proficiency of a chef that was recognized in a great writer, musician, or artist. It was the attention to minute details that elevated any craft to an art form, and whether a sonata, sculpture, or sorbet, there was little difference. Diver set to task with his tubers. As he did, he pined over the critic Donald Kuspit's latest article in Artnet Magazine. It posed a question to all young artists: "Why make art?" The difficulty of answering lied in a prohibition on myth making, which Diver had always presumed Kuspit associated with tropes. Saving the world. Bridging cultures. Healing wounds. These were not acceptable answers, nor were they sufficiently personalized to be meaningful. When in art school, Diver remembered it being a question seldom asked by instructors. As if the cart were leading the horse, the reasons for art making went unaddressed, perhaps for fear of losing students. He remembered a question his former professor once asked: "Did the world *need* more art?" It was a reasonable question. The world was, after all, quite full already. "Most of you will simply contribute to landfills," the professor would follow, to the shock of the young faces in the room. It was several years after this that Diver read Annie Dillard's plea for young writers to seek new careers for their own sanity's sake.

What was this self-mockery that seemed essential to creative activity? Was it deflection, self-preservation, preclusion? Whatever the correct response (if there was a correct response), Diver sought to change the question. Whether or not the world needed more art, it certainly seemed to need a primer in what it means to be a human being. For Diver, that meant paying as much attention to potato turning as to child rearing or to nation building. If all things require the correct attention, no things are left unattended.

To that end, Diver had co-signed loan documents for Lanny's longtime dream, The Family Kitchen, one week before. While his success at *De Terre* was noted in his small community, it was not highly profitable, even with Diver co-owning and residing in the building. Were Diver more concerned with profit, he could have made more, but profit too frequently comes at the expense of one's neighbors. Even though Diver chose not to live a social life, it did not mean he didn't still believe in society, however hard that was from day to day. But with Lanny the decision was easy. Diver always liked his idea — not only did it encourage a return to simply made nutritious food, but also provided two or three hours a week of sacred time between a parent and child not otherwise easily shared in the tumult of post-modern life. Far from being a high-stakes backer, Diver was able to deposit ten thousand dollars into Lanny's business account with little care for a lucrative return. If there was any hope left for the world, may it be born in cheese-making classes everywhere.

After the last of the fingerlings floated delicately in the Pyrex bowl, Diver looked up at the clock. One hour to opening, and now time for the quiche. He knew that's what Claire would order.

Nine

A good quiche starts with the crust. But few pay attention to the pan in which the crust is baked. Diver used a preheated, heavy cast-iron skillet to bake the simple but hearty dough, giving its edges a crisp buttery varnish intensified with the addition of cheese.

Adding flour and salt to a stainless bowl, Diver proceeded to cut two pounds of cold butter into small pieces of roughly uniform size. Once complete, he added two teaspoons of fresh sage and a handful of shredded white cheddar to the bowl and mixed the dry ingredients with a quick whisk of his hand. Mounting two butter knives into the closed knuckles of his left hand, he added pats of cold butter to the flour mix slowly, chopping it into the dry mix with quick repetitive strokes. Scraping and moving the bowl in his right arm, the mix, now having all the butter added, soon turned to a beaded mass of marble-sized flour pellets.

Diver set the bowl down and added several tablespoons of cold water to the mix, turning it out onto a chilled piece of marble. He worked it with his hands until the mix incorporated itself into a large ball of dough. After rolling the sphere several times over the stone to compact it, he sat in on the top shelf of the reach-in beneath a sheet of wax paper.

Increasingly, his disgust with the world darkened his mood. He could not ignore the lack of justice amongst the powerful, who made daily choices concerning those who lived and who died, or more inconspicuously, those who lived well and those who suffered. If any god had ever cared for humans, that care had ended long ago. If postmodernity was marked by the absence of heroes, then those heroes who remained would now be defined by their inadequacies. The villains had become too strong.

Why was it necessary for Siddhartha to leave human society to achieve enlightenment? Because the earth was permanently stained. A miasma of our own making. And amidst that pollution Diver found some solace, or perhaps sublimation, in attacking himself. He had developed ticks, one of which was to pull his hair out; the other was to bite his skin. Diver met the violence of the world by turning violence upon himself. To answer the question of what it means to be a human being, Diver could not ignore the fact that any response must address our predilection to cruelty.

He then began skinning and dicing an eggplant. After finishing, he dumped the cubes into a bowl of seasoned flour and minced two cloves of garlic with the white flesh of a leek. Leaving his mise en place for a moment, he walked to the pantry and brought back a small jar of sun-dried tomatoes cured in oil. Quickly he dumped its contents through a sieve, transferring the red oil to a heavy-bottomed saucepan. In a moment, the oil in the pan began warming atop the front burner of the range.

Leeks figure prominently in Carolyn Forche's *Angel of History.* In her haunting poem of postwar Europe, beautifully terse yet warm descriptions of food and flowers act as beacons of life surrounded by omnipresent specters of death. Diver recalled one of his favorite phrases:

> *In the café across from Zivnostenská banka we are able to buy*
> *a sack of bread for the road, and poppies*

In the tin light we walk, our sandwiches in foil
Like the night along Národni, street of the kiosks
The wind has eaten the faces from the angels of Charles Bridge
As if the earth were finished with us
We leave our konvalinka for the saint, white tulips for the
mother of God.

The blood of man is compost to growing things. Diver loved her writing, which was smart and sharp as a knife. She made words somehow corporal, and was proof that great despair and powerlessness was best met with the simplest acts: a walk, a gesture, an embrace, or a meal. These acts of humility could be the greatest answers to violence, but their elegance seemed far beyond our biology. This juxtaposition plagued Diver like a malignant nightmare. Was his response to violence the act of sharing food? Or was it the act of turning the violence upon himself?

When Diver's oil expanded and glistened from the heat, he tossed the small, floured cubes of eggplant into the pan, watching them bubble instantly. In two minutes they were fried golden brown, and he removed to rest on a stack of paper towels to soak the excess grease and cool to room temperature.

Market flowers in a jar, a string of tied garlic, and a voice
moving off as if fearing itself.

A phrase so apt for Diver, describing one present in sensory experience yet desirous of absence, always trailing away from contact. He had been that way for some time now, increasingly courting solitude as the days grew shorter. When not cooking he was reading, when not reading he looked silently up to his dark ceiling while lying in bed wishing for sleep.

Violence. Art. Onions. War. Tulips. And now quiche. Perhaps labor is the diversion we need to not scream. Diver pressed the cold moist dough around the circumference of his large cast-iron skillet. It was 16 inches in diameter and weighed 45 pounds — a true behemoth at three inches deep. After covering the base of the skillet, Diver poked holes into the dough with a fork and lit a burner beneath it, leaving it on low heat. In a bowl he mixed the leeks and garlic, previously sautéed, with sun-dried tomatoes, warm chevre and the fried eggplant. Adding 20 eggs and some milk, he folded the mix together with sea salt and white pepper, and warmed it over a double boiler. He then folded in six egg whites beaten to soft peaks. When he poured his custard into the skillet, it rose to the top of the crust. Seventy-five minutes and 350 degrees later, one of *De Terre's* most popular daily specials would be ready to serve.

And with quiche might come a bit of hope. No extra charge.

Ten

At night we ride through mansions of glory in suicide machines.
— Bruce Springsteen

As Claire pulled into the driveway of the brick garage apartment, Elizabeth, a tall willowy brunette, skipped up to the Honda's passenger door. Her best friend of two years, Liz was a doctoral student majoring in classical languages, and she'd shared several graduate classes with Claire in the last year. She was older than Claire, but Claire gravitated to persons older than her. Their date that night was for dinner, wherein Claire hoped to recruit Liz for the *De Terre* book club.

"Hey, Claire," Liz greeted happily. She splashed into the car seat like a wave of auburn cotton, her hair loosely falling over a tight brown cashmere top.

"Hi, Liz, " Claire replied, looking over the car seat. "Whew, it's cold out tonight, are you sure you don't want something more than that sweater?"

"First cold night of the year. I want to feel the brisk."

"Sure you just don't want your boobs to pop?"

"Clever girl." Liz smirked.

Claire drove out of the driveway and down the street before turning on Main. It was a small town, made smaller by its centralized business district.

Winter had crept in early, it seemed. Only mid-October, morning frosts had become common, if only for the several hours before midday. The sun awoke a bit later every morning, and evenings came quicker and darker and quieter. Midterms were right around the corner, and soon thereafter, the holidays.

"My mom is Facebooking now," Liz said with rolling eyes. "I spent two hours today teaching her how to tag people."

"Ugh, now you'll get messages every day."

"I'm not worried about that so much as I am her getting her identity stolen. Last month she opened an email and downloaded a porn bomb. It maxed out her memory. She had to call the geek squad."

"Was it any good?"

"The porn?" Liz asked incredulously.

"Yeah. Maybe your mom did it on purpose."

Liz shook her head and winced. "Gross, Claire. Just gross."

Soon after, they entered *De Terre's* small parking lot. "This is the place," Claire said, switching off her ignition.

"I'm excited," Liz replied, "and hungry."

They opened the restaurant door and walked inside. As they did, Lanny looked up from the bar and nodded to Claire, who waived back. He approached them and told them to seat themselves wherever they liked.

"Let's sit by the fireplace," Liz said.

They walked to and sat at a cozy table beside the fire, which only glowed with embers. It was quite enough to warm the slight chill in the evening air. Prior to a front moving through, it had been a warm day, surely one of the few remaining in the year's calendar.

Once they sat, Lanny approached the table with menus and water for their glasses. A group of four diners sat beside them to the left, who were conversing quietly in good humor.

"Good evening, Claire," Lanny greeted. "How are you tonight?"

"Good, Lanny. Thank you. How are you?"

"Good. It's been a slow one. Let me take care of this table's check and I'll be right over to chat."

Liz glanced at the single-page typewritten menu. "Oh, my god, they have hominy. Who serves hominy? I love hominy. I think I must have been a Mayan or something in a former life."

Claire smiled. "Reincarnation? That's not very scientific."

"I'm not sure of that," Liz replied. "Think about it, nature wastes nothing. I think there's an ecological argument to be made in favor of it. If matter cannot be created, than what the hell is a baby anyway? Some kind of reconstituted cellular has-been, right?"

"Some would call it a miracle."

"Well, I'm joking anyway. I don't believe in reincarnation. At the end of the day, it's just vanity. Like all religions. We don't want to imagine nonbeing once we've been."

"That sounds more like the Liz I know," Claire said with a smile. "Anyway, the menu's terrific. Everything is good, but I usually have the quiche."

"All right then, on to more exciting topics…like this guy. Where is Mr. Chef?"

Claire blushed. "He doesn't know I'm alive," she whispered sheepishly, smacking Liz's wrist. "And shush! Lanny will hear you."

"Hear what, ladies?" Lanny interjected, walking briskly to their table.

"Hear us gossiping," Liz answered.

"Believe me, in this job, I've heard it all. Who's your friend, Claire?"

"Lanny, this is Liz. Liz, this is Lanny."

"Very nice to meet you, Liz. Can I get your glass of wine on the house? It's a tradition for first-timers."

"I'd love a pinot. Do you have anything from Oregon?"

Lanny grinned. "The lady knows her geography."

"Lanny's a wine snob, Liz. You've just endeared yourself to him."

"I only know a few tricks," Liz retorted, "so don't think too much of me. I'm on a student budget after all."

"Knowing labels can be overwhelming. Knowing regions is easier. And keep track of the amount of rain they get. Drier seasons are always better for wine. I have some favorites. For instance, if you're going Italian think Lazio for white and Piedmont for reds. Same thing with France, although I don't like French wines as much as others. Stay with the Côte D'Azur, Châteauneuf-du-Pape. Not far from that is La Rioja in Spain. The latitude is practically the same."

"What about the good old USA? Liz queried, "You know, buy American and all."

"If you're not going with the pinot, then it's really all about zinfandel. People don't think about it because there's so much sweet stuff out there. But I think it's what California does best. There are a few chardonnays around, too, not so bitter as most. The Finger Lakes have some good rieslings now."

"Good to know, Lanny. ...So what recommendation do you have for me?"

"I have two Oregon pinots this week. Wallace Brook, which has a bit of brightness on the tongue with some citrus, and Elk Cove, which is deeper and more complex."

"I'm thinking the Wallace," she ordered. "Thank you."

"And for you, Claire?" Lanny asked, pen in hand.

"I'll have my usual, Lanny."

"The Rioja?'

"Yes, indeed. I'm nothing if not loyal."

"I'll be right back, ladies." Lanny bowed and gestured, before exiting the table to the bar.

De Terre was not particularly crowded that night. Two other tables were seated besides their own, each already eating. Liz and Claire frequently ate late, the result of evening classes. Truth was, they were night owls, which added to their immediate synchronicity. While Claire was the more conservative of the two, they had so much in common that they became very close very quickly.

"Back to my question, Claire," Liz prodded. "Who is this chef?"

"His name is John," Claire replied. "He's a little older, a little jaded, and a big mystery."

"Ahhhhh," Liz goaded, "Claire wants to unravel a mystery!"

"He might be too much of one I fear." Claire sighed. "He's not a particularly open person."

"Every man is a clam, Claire, you just need to shuck him."

"We'll see," she answered. "Right now you just be supportive...and quietly so."

Before Liz could retort, Lanny returned to the table with two long-stemmed glasses of deep red wine. "One Rioja," he stated as he placed the glass in front of Claire, "and one Pinot for our newest regular."

"Thank you, Lanny," Claire said. She swirled her glass and watched its legs cling delicately to the vessel before disappearing.

Liz swallowed a small mouthful. "Mmmmm," she chimed, "delicious. Excellent recommendation."

"Thank you," Lanny answered with a smile. "Regarding our menu tonight. Our soup is a tomato Champagne, served a room temperature. And, Claire, if I may say, John has prepared his quiche with you in mind. I mentioned you were coming in.

"She's nothing if not loyal," Liz mimicked. "And I'll have the same. Can we have the cheese plate to start?"

"Absolutely. Tonight we have a caraway Havarti, a triple-cream goat cheese and a homemade raw milk mozzarella with local rhubarb preserves."

"That sounds great."

"I'll be just a few minutes," Lanny offered. "My others tables are finished. After that, I'm all yours."

As he walked away, Liz giggled. "He looks like Lewis Black," she smiled sheepishly.

"Younger," Claire agreed, "but with tighter curls and more hair."

"And less jowl." They both laughed and drank. "To our future." Liz toasted.

"To our future," Claire agreed. "And to ski season!"

"Yes! To hell with the library."

Soon afterward, Lanny arrived and laid a handsome cheese plate down between the two ladies. He placed two small forks at either side of the tray, and refilled their water glasses.

"Two more glasses of wine?" he asked, noting each stem less than half full.

"Indeed. No morning classes tomorrow."

"Extra cheese on your quiche, Claire?"

"Thanks, Lanny," she replied.

"And you, Liz?"

"Sounds perfect."

"I'll put the orders in now, unless you prefer to wait?"

"No, bring it forth, good sir." Claire responded.

Liz swallowed. "I'd think you'd want to milk it, Claire. It's not everyday a chef makes you a quiche, for goodness sake."

Claire sipped her wine. "There's always a quiche of the day, Liz. And I always order it."

"Even so. He made tonight's special for you."

"That's Lanny playing matchmaker. He thinks he's subtle."

Liz smiled. "So what's his story?"

"I'm not sure. Lanny's been here for a while. I know he wants to open his own business. John is helping him, I think. He's usually not here in the afternoon for our reading group, so I only see him during dinner."

"He's gay, right?"

"I think so. I haven't exactly come out and asked him."

"That's pretty tough in this podunk town. He must be lonely."

At that moment, the *De Terre's* front door opened, always noticeable by the warm sound of four bells attached to the top of the jamb ringing joyfully upon entry. In walked Simon Pence, felted gray fedora in hand, shaking the evening chill off his slight frame. Claire smiled at him, noticing he was alone.

"I know him," she said, turning to Liz. "He's in the reading group."

"Invite him over," Liz replied. "It'll give me some insight into this group you want me to join...let me do some recon."

"Are you sure?" Claire asked.

"Sure," Liz answered. "He looks classy."

"He is."

Claire waived at Simon, who walked to the table to greet her.

"Why, good evening, Claire," he addressed.

"Hi, Simon. How are you tonight?"

"A bit peckish," he replied with a smile.

Claire introduced her friends. "Simon, this is my good friend Liz."

"A pleasure to meet you, Elizabeth," Simon gestured, taking and kissing her right hand.

"The pleasure is mine," Liz offered, clearly charmed.

"Will you join us? We've ordered, but Lanny can hold it. We're in no hurry."

"I should never refuse the company of two lovely women," Simon accepted. He turned around momentarily and placed his hat upon the rack at the door before returning to Claire and Liz.

"Hello, Simon, it's nice to see you again. Three times this week," Lanny said warmly, as he pulled a chair to the amply sized two-top. The restaurant was now theirs, the other tables having left moments ago. "Seven and seven?"

"Yes, please. And I'll have the soup tonight."

"Tonight's is a cold soup, but I think John has potato leek left from yesterday. Would you like that instead?"

"That sounds splendid."

As Lanny left to procure the cocktail, Simon slowly reclined into the padded oak chair.

As he did, in the back John simmered a reduction in a heavy saucepan, glancing up at the clock on the wall. It was 8:55

p.m. He began to think about breaking down the kitchen for the night.

Just one table left.

Eleven

"How did you come to the group, Simon?" Claire asked.

"Well, I'll tell you a secret, Dear," he replied, "John and I are partners."

Claire's eyes widened. "I had no idea."

"I just helped with some seed money really. But as for your question about the reading group, that requires a different answer."

"What?"

"A bit of a long story really. Jacob was my wife's nurse. She was diagnosed with cancer a few years back. Both breasts. Late stage. Jacob would come to see her several days a week in our home. She hated hospitals."

"I'm so sorry, Simon." Liz offered.

"Thank you," Simon said. "She died four years ago. She passed like she wanted to, with her dignity and at home, not tied to a machine. I would cook for her and read to her most every night. That's how I got to know Jacob, and then Bill."

"A terrible way to meet, but life is so strange that way," Liz said awkwardly.

Simon sipped his drink and shook the ice in the glass. "Indeed. My Josie knew long before any of us that her time would be short. She kept her spirits up. And Jacob, too. He's a good man."

"You've never mentioned that."

"I guess you're right," Simon replied. "To us its old and unfortunate history. No need to be spoken. Truth is, I've little in common with them other than that, particularly with Bill. And now I guess the reading group."

"Claire tells me you need another woman. You know, for balance."

Simon smiled. "I'm not sure Bill wants balance. It would mean less time in the spotlight."

"Oh, he's not that bad," Claire joked.

"No, that's true, but there are times I wonder if he's read anything past the 1800s."

"That sounds like my kind of man," Liz said. "I'm a classicist."

"Oh, dear. That would make two of you then," Simon said with a grin. "What are your likes?"

"I like the Greeks, mostly because they were such a sordid lot. I'm doing work on Epicurus."

"I've not heard of him."

"You're not alone. He liked pleasure."

"Few men don't," Simon replied.

"Well, Dante wasn't pleased. He wrote him into the sixth circle of hell in his *Inferno*. I'm actually writing a piece of fiction about it."

"A writer, too," Simon replied, "Good for you, Dear."

"But to change the topic slightly," Liz interjected, "how does the group choose readings?'

"At first, before Claire joined, we did themes. That got a bit tedious. Now we take turns. Each member gets to choose one book per month. Anything goes."

"What was yours, Claire?"

"I told you," Claire stated incredulously, "*A Room of One's Own*. Virginia Woolf."

"A good text," Simon shared, "I enjoyed every page. I must say your presence has made for a richer conversation, Claire. I'm glad you seem to be comfortable with old men."

Claire smiled. She, too, was glad. Sometimes she felt more comfortable with her reading group than with adults her own age. They took more time to think before speaking. She took a deep gulp of her wine, finishing it, knowing she would have another.

Lanny popped into the kitchen to smell the aromatic reduction John was finishing with a swirl of whole butter.

"Claire's here, John, with a friend. And Simon, too."

John looked up from the burner.

"They came together?"

"Not with Simon. They just joined each other in the dining room."

John smiled. "Good for them. Have they ordered?"

Lanny crossed his arms up on the pass through separating him from the line. "Claire's having the usual, along with her friend. And Simon would like a bowl of yesterday's potato leek. Is that OK?"

"Sure." John offered back. "So who's her friend?"

"Her roommate. She seems nice. Tall. Pretty. Wants her quiche with extra cheese."

"Claire mentioned her to me before. I think she's wanting her to join the reading group."

"Right you are," Lanny replied. "That happens to be the subject of their conversation."

"All right," said John, wiping his hands on his apron. "How's their timing? I can have that out anytime."

"They had a cheese plate. They're ready, but don't seem to be in any hurry. Besides they're our last table. I say take your time. They're drinking."

"Perhaps it's that time for me, too, then," John said.

"Do you want something? I'm going to check on their drinks."

"I have some Sam Adams in the cooler. I'd love one when you come back."

"Sure thing, Chef."

"Thanks."

"No problem. And you know, John, you should come out and say hi to your guests."

As Lanny left and swept through the door, he heard the women laughing at the table. It made him smile to know they were having a good time. That was enough. There was no need to join.

"What do you like to read, Simon?" Liz asked in an animated fashion.

Before he could reply, Lanny returned with a new round of drinks. Simon could tell he was a few behind his companions.

"To new friends," Simon toasted calmly.

"To new friends," they replied.

They drank together. "As to your question, Elizabeth, I'm rather old-fashioned. I like the classics. Dickens. Steinbeck. Twain."

Claire interrupted. "Oh! A friend of mine is getting her doctorate in American literature. She's doing her dissertation on Twain."

"A woman of good taste," Simon returned. "What is her thesis?"

"I'm not sure," she stated, "but it's focused on his critiques of American politics."

"Good for her."

"What do you do, Simon?" Liz continued, "I mean, when you're not reading the classics."

"I was a geography teacher for seventeen years. Before that, I worked in the Air Force, teaching cartography to reservists. Today, I am retired."

"Simon is the last of the Buckley conservatives, Liz," Claire chuckled.

Following this last exchange, Lanny came to the table with their meals. He placed an oversized bowl of soup before Simon, before placing the quiche with the women. "Sorry, ladies. I know you should be served first, but giant bowls of hot soup get me nervous."

"It does look rather steamy," Claire acknowledged.

Simon smiled. "John knows I like my soup very hot. He always remembers. It's the little things."

"Where is this mystery man?" Liz asked, looking around at the empty restaurant. "Can he come out and say hi?"

"I'll see," Lanny replied, "if I can drag him out of his kitchen."

Claire took her first bite of the moist casserole, tasting the herbs and rich eggs all at once. "Oh, my. This is amazing," she said, almost humming. "How's your soup?"

With his perfect manners, Simon took a moment before replying after sipping. "It's wonderful, Claire. But—" Simon added with a whisper, "it could use some meat, of course."

Liz laughed. "You're in the wrong place for that."

"I keep hoping I can turn our chef to the dark side. A juicy, succulent dark side."

"Do you know why John's a vegetarian, Claire?" Liz asked.

"No. I've never asked." She poked at her plate. "The truth is, I don't know much about him."

Simon turned to Claire and said warmly, "None of us do, Dear. But it strikes me that you'd like to know more."

"Claire's got a crush," Liz half-whispered. "She wants the chef special."

"Liz!"

Simon chuckled softly. "You need not be embarrassed. I had sensed as much last week."

"How?"

"An old man is not always wise, but most often he's observant. The world slows down for him."

"My goodness, you are a charmer. Did you just walk off the silver screen?" Liz sighed.

"My dear, the world needs more love stories today than it ever has. Don't be afraid to follow your heart."

Claire blushed. "We'll see. But how about you, Simon? How did you meet Josephine?"

"My Josie," Simon answered, "We were married thirty-seven years -- so long that I can't remember the days before I met her. It was at a drive-in movie, of all things. We were both their with different groups of people. We met at the soda stand — that was back when they had intermissions. I knew her brother from the college prep squad. We chatted a few minutes. She bought a pop, but was twenty cents short. I loaned it to her. She said she'd come back at the end of the movie to pay me back. And so I waited for her. And now I imagine she's waiting for me to join her…she and my son."

Claire touched his hand and choked up. "Simon."

"Let's turn to you, Dear. To the young. Your life lies before you an endless road."

"I'm stuck in neutral, I'm afraid," Claire said sheepishly, lifting a forkful of quiche to her lips.

"Life has a way of putting you in drive," Simon replied. "Three years ago, I was quietly awaiting death. A man with nothing keeping him on the Earth."

"What happened?" Liz asked.

Simon smiled. "And now we are back to my first reveal. That's when I became partners with John." Simon turned his chair and pointed to the brick wall behind them. "And it all began with that wall," he said, pointing to *De Terre's* famed façade.

"The wall?" Liz replied.

"My father built that wall," Simon continued. "They were going to tear this place down. Cheaper to rebuild than restore. It's happening all over the country. No sense of history." Simon stopped to butter a warm roll before continuing. "That's how I met John. He was in the library when I came in for some records. He knew this building and had been keeping his eyes on it for this restaurant. We talked a bunch and formed a plan. We fought together to keep this place alive. He helped get the preservation board behind it. One day I was sitting at home and he called me, saying he had found the construction records for the building. He asked me if I was related to a Leopold Pence. I told him that was my father."

"Wow," Claire interjected.

"Wow indeed," Simon replied smiling, "Well, ultimately the city denied our landmark status. But over that three months, John and I got to know each other pretty well. We became business partners. And now we own this building together."

"Double wow." Liz added.

"That's how we met," Simon continued, "and that's how I learned to love vegetables."

"What a cool story," Liz replied, reaching for her wine glass.

"Well, the truth is," Simon added after a pause, "I distrust vegetables, but I love that man. He rescued a piece of my father. And of me. And I do not believe that it is mere coincidence that we met shortly after my son died. Life works in mysterious ways."

At that moment, John swung through the revolving door to the kitchen with beer in hand and walked to the table smiling.

"Hello, Simon. Hello, Claire. How are your meals?"

"Wonderful," Claire responded, putting down her fork and shifting her hair behind an ear. "John, this is my friend, Liz."

"Hello, Liz," John responded. "Welcome."

"Thanks, John. Claire has told me a lot about you. She loves your food."

"I'm very happy to hear that."

"Why don't you come sit with us. You're done for the night, yes?"

"Well, I've a few things…"

Simon interrupted. "Please sit down with us, John. Have another glass of beer."

John sighed. "Let me go get a snack. I usually eat after the dinner rush. I'll be right back and I'll sit down with you." He turned to the kitchen, asking Lanny, who has at the bar, for another beer as he left.

In the kitchen he grabbed a few slices of bread and placed them on his flat top to toast. He turned off all the equipment on the line before he grabbed some Swiss cheese out of his reach-in and cut several thin slices. He then sliced an avocado and a tomato, and stacked the ingredients between the bread to make a sandwich. He downed most of his pint with great gulps and belched. Oddly, he found himself rushing to return to the dining room.

As he swung back out to the front of the house, his last table was laughing and talking jovially.

"As promised," Diver said before sitting down. Lanny had poured a new beer at his place setting. John took another healthy swig. He turned to Lanny. "I do like this new winter lager."

"Its nice to have you sit with us, John," Simon began. We were just talking about dancing. People don't dance anymore. I think it's a failing of society. These two young women have never been fox-trotted."

"That sounds dirty, Simon," Liz chuckled.

Claire looked over at Diver. "John," she said incredulously, "you're having a cheese sandwich for dinner?"

Claire caught John taking a bite. He looked up sheepishly and smirked. After chewing quickly he replied. "This is one of my favorite things in the world. Swiss cheese, tomato and avocado. I've been eating it for years."

"Seems rather pedestrian," Liz answered.

"A workingman's meal," Simon retorted. "Lots of protein."

"The truth is," John answered, "the last thing I want to do after working all night is to cook for myself. This is my go-to stomach stuffer."

Acting as Claire's wingman, Liz then had a thought. "Simon," she said slyly, "Will you show me the wall that your father built? You peaked my interest earlier."

"Surely. Excuse us please." Simon gestured to the table, before rising and taking Liz's arm, walking her to the other side of the restaurant.

"She seems very nice," John offered to Claire, watching the pair walk away.

"She's the best," Claire responded, "Smart. Sure of herself. Serious when she needs to be. Funny the rest of the time."

At that moment John took in Claire for the first time that evening. She wore a green dress with black tights. A gold necklace sparkled on her exposed neck. Her hair has down, which was unusual for her, and she was looking at him with a long stare. Not quite adoringly. But not shy either.

"The food was delicious tonight, John. Let me ask. Do you ever let someone cook for you? I feel like you cook for me all the time."

John felt warm. He took a few swallows of his Sam Adams. "Truth is," he admitted, "I don't even really cook for me. I like to cook for other people. When the time comes, I usually just have the easiest thing around."

"I'm not as great as you, but maybe you'd let me make you dinner sometime. My mom taught me some good recipes." Claire smiled and looked down at the table when she met John's eyes.

Suddenly, John realized they were flirting. It had been so long—not that he was used to it in the first place—but her attention now expressed itself to him in ways he had never really believed could happen. Claire Dankowski, a young, intelligent and graceful woman was offering to cook him dinner. Diver scanned his mental Rolodex of citations—to whom should he refer? Fitzgerald? O'Connor? He was suddenly without context, unarmored, forced to live in the moment by the overwhelming embrace of sincerity, by a risk of the heart, by life laid open before him. He was not able to scour the endnotes. This conversation was in real time.

Claire's red hair danced just over the top of her brown eyes. She was slightly freckled, and her cheeks now were reddened more than usual. Diver offered himself to the moment. "I'll tell you what," he said, "let's say we open a bottle of wine. I'll lock the door and put a log on the fire. And we enjoy tonight before it ends."

Claire lifted her empty glass. "You had me at wine."

Twelve

It could be this easy to love you. It could be this easy for undestructed helpings of budding day to stack themselves up against an onslaught of light.

— Ariana Reines

Postmodern artists see the world in all its naked tragedy. They dissect it not in the abstract, like a realm of one's imagination, but in the sweaty musk of human flesh. Diver never recognized this as much as in that moment, sitting three feet from the woman making his throat swell and his back sweat. He needed Celine. He needed Bukowski. He needed Reines. He needed the courage to be vulnerable, the audacity to believe, and a healthy indifference to failure. In short, he needed to be fully present.

But first he needed more wine.

Within a few moments, he inventoried the bar and gathered several water glasses and a bottle of Chianti. He walked them all back to Claire.

De Terre was theirs.

"So, John Diver," Liz began as Diver popped the red stained cork. "What do you think of this reading group? I'm being recruited." She and Simon rejoined the pair with the arrival of the wine.

"They're a good bunch," Diver replied, as Lanny also walked over to the table.

"They could tip better," Lanny joked, leaning down to grab a glass. "John, I'm going to balance out and head home. My back is acting up again."

"Won't you stay for a bit, Lanny?" Claire invited.

"Sorry, Claire. I have a date with an aspirin and a hardwood floor. Besides, I'm your fifth wheel." That said, he toasted the group and began counting out the register behind the bar.

"I guess that means we're on our first date, Simon," Liz smiled.

"And perhaps us, too." Claire said softly looking at John.

"Then we are both lucky men," Simon stated proudly, nodding to John.

Lanny counted out the till in the register. *De Terre* was not computerized. John had complete trust in Lanny's accounting skills. He relied on him to balance the handwritten checks in a black ledger book, recording each night's gross before placing the funds into a small but heavy cast-iron safe that looked like an antique. Diver would later use the checks to assess the number of sales by entrée so that he could keep track of his guest's choices. Diver would make deposits to the bank every other morning and on Fridays. It was a fairly simple system, made possible by their modest amount of business. *De Terre* was consistently profitable, but in a most humble way. Theirs was not a venue of three hundred covers a night. In all the time Lanny had been with John, he had never deposited more than twelve hundred dollars and never less than four hundred dollars in the safe at any one time.

He looked over to the four-top engaged in conversation. It made Lanny happy to see John out of the kitchen. He placed a rubber band around the night's take and dropped it into the safe.

That night he had made fifty-four dollars in tips, which bulged out of his front pocket as he reached for the ledger to record the evening's numbers.

"These two are the base, the foundation of any topical conversation," John returned to Liz pointing to Simon and Claire, "Bill and Jacob, well...Bill really...he adds a certain loftiness. If you can stand it, that is. And Jacob is the quieter of the two, often playing the straight man to his brother. But he is very well-read, too."

"We need another woman, Liz," Claire stated again. "We have to balance things out. We're reading too many men." As she said the last phrase the chime of Lanny's register echoed in the background.

Liz continued, her lips loosened from the wine. "But don't you sit in, too, John? Claire tells me you've read everything."

"But then who would cook for you? Thinking burns calories, you know."

Claire rolled her eyes. "He sits in sometimes, Liz. Don't let him fool you."

"Who do you like to read?" Liz pressed.

Diver took a long drink of the Chianti and paused a moment. "Really, I like lots of things. History, especially. Thucydides. Aeschylus. I like raw stuff, like Cormac McCarthy and Pinckney Benedict."

"No women there, John," Liz continued. "Do you not read women?"

John smiled. "You got me. Allow me to add to my list. Sheila Heti. Karen Russell. Toni Morrison."

"Well played, Chef" Liz smiled. She then turned to Claire. "I think I can work with him."

Claire seemed happy. "Do you realize he's told you more about himself in the last hour than he has to me in two months?"

John looked at Claire. "I'm sorry, Claire." He breathed. "It's your turn then. Ask me anything."

The moment he said it he regretted it. He had opened himself. His neck was suddenly cold. He felt himself biting the inside of his cheek.

After a pause, Liz rose. "This sounds like a private conversation, Simon," she whispered. "Let's go help Lanny so he can get home."

With that, the two strode quietly over to the bar. Liz put Simon's fedora on her head playfully. "This is vintage. The hipsters would be jealous."

Simon glanced at John and smiled. It was the glance of a father to his son.

Claire renewed her intensity. She put down her glass. "OK, John, it's just us. Last week, you told me your greatest fear was failing at life. What did you mean?"

Diver glanced over at the wall, which offered no encouragement. He looked down at the table, and then up to Claire's eyes, which were glistening ever so slightly in the low light. It was time to actually share something.

"I'll be honest, Claire. Well, you've probably noticed I don't talk a lot. I've never been very relaxed around people. I'm not quite *sure* why, but I think I know the answer," John said. He glanced at Claire, who nodded for him to continue. "I've never really been comfortable in this world. And I don't mean that I belong to another," John said, using his hands to wave off that idea. "I'm talking about the systems we've created. The social structures. Economic structures. Class structures. I just don't understand life. Not the how, I get that, but rather the *why*. Why human beings have built this system. And it's a system I can't buy into. We've built it over thousands of years, across the entire world. Which makes me think *I'm* the odd man out. I'm the one failing. I'm the one who just doesn't…get it."

When he finished speaking, John realized it had been easier to express himself than he had thought. But once done, he had nothing left to say.

The room seemed oddly silent.

Claire leaned across the table. John thought she was about to whisper something, when, to his surprise, she boldly pressed her face to his and kissed him on the cheek, just off his mouth. It was soft but wet. Assured but gentle.

That was her answer to him.

Thirteen

Claire had been cleaning her living room for three hours. It was clean an hour ago, but she kept going anyway. The university apartment she lived in was reserved for graduate students. It was a bit nicer, a bit more spacious, and removed from campus. In fact, it appeared more like a small, privately owned townhouse than anything. It was included with her scholarship, as were the utilities. In exchange, Claire worked fifteen hours per week in the central library. She re-shelved books in the afternoons.

She was surprised when John admitted to her that, despite popular belief, he was not exclusively a vegetarian and would sometimes eat seafood. He had agreed to dinner last week, and she desired to cook him something memorable. She was baking salmon with fresh dill and celery seed, a favorite Sunday meal of her mother's. The mild scent wafted through the kitchen, married with the sweet woody smell of beeswax candles on the table. The fish was twenty minutes away. The brown rice was just coming off the stovetop. A plate of fresh tomatoes and pickled red onions cooled in the refrigerator.

As her doorbell rang, she took one last look at herself in the mirror that hung in the hallway by the entryway. She took a deep breath and opened the door.

"Hi, Claire," John began, a bottle of wine in his hands.

"Hi. Welcome. Please come in."

Diver had been standing outside the door for about ninety seconds before ringing the bell, although it seemed like ninety minutes. His feet were heavy and his palms were sweating. He had urinated four times in the last hour. He had thought of not going, thought of hiding up in his small room above *De Terre* where he watched the world revolve around him. He had made sure to get good and drunk the night before, wallowing in an essay written by Anthony Burgess.

Is freedom of choice really all that important? For that matter, is man capable of it? Again, does the term "freedom" have any intrinsic meaning?

Burgess, in a diversion from his topic of *The Clockwork Orange* (although perhaps not a diversion at all) was speaking to the role of the state in the conditioning of the mind, which, Diver interpreted, is made easier by our natural propensity to conformity, ramped up on steroids through decades of commercial marketing. Are we enslaved more by Coca-Cola than any totalitarian regime could hope for? It was a robust, if not mildly exaggerated, dialectic; however, the answer was not forthcoming to Diver even after his six ounces of bourbon.

What was more significant that night was the micro rather than the macro. Diver meditated on *his* freedom of choice. He realized that he was being drawn to Claire in a way that he could not define. That he could not articulate. His immediate reaction to this was to nurture his recalcitrance — to seek and define the many reasons he should forgo their dinner. Intellectually speaking, he had no reason to be there. But there he was, wine in hand, staring blankly at the white aluminum door like it held a secret he could only learn by entering. He wondered if he had any choice at all.

Diver handed Claire the bottle of white. "I think you'll like this. It's very buttery."

"Let me take your coat, John," Claire replied. "Then you can open it for us."

John handed Claire his jacket and looked into the living room, walking slowly. "Your apartment is nice. It's big."

"I'm lucky," she replied, moving beside him. "It's more than I need."

Claire and John both felt a slight awkwardness permeate the room. John looked into the kitchen.

"Electric stove?" he asked.

Claire walked to the wall cabinet, taking two wine glasses. "Unfortunately, yes. It not the greatest either."

She looked at John, who stood in the doorjamb of the kitchen, the light hitting his face clearly. His brown hair was a bit windswept. He was wearing a light-blue dress shirt in need of a pressing. She could tell he did not dress up frequently, but he had made an effort for her. She liked that.

My god, he reminds me of my dad, she thought. *Is this the fate of all women?*

Claire grinned at him. "Want to pop it?" she said, handing John an opener.

As Diver opened the bottle and poured the chilled chardonnay, Claire continued.

"I was going to play some music, but I remembered you don't prefer it."

John handed Claire a glass. They drank together.

"Mmm," Claire responded, puckering her lips, "and Lanny says there are no good chardonnays."

Her joke broke the ice. Diver smirked. "Lanny is not often wrong about wine. I'll have to tell him about this one." He walked into the living room, just beyond her reach. "Some music would be nice, Claire. What do you like to listen to?"

"Most things really…except the new country stuff. Oh, and metal…yuck." She smirked and looked comfortingly at John, "I'll put on something quiet."

"Whatever you'd like, please." John gestured.

As he watched Claire finger through her ungainly CD collection, he swallowed a large gulp of wine, which was just opening nicely. From it, a few cool beads of condensation ran onto to his hands. Diver hoped Claire did not notice the sweat on his back. He was vulnerable. He imagined at any moment she would regain her senses and laugh him out the door. He felt like he was the unknowing buffoon in a hidden-camera reality show.

He began gnawing on the inside of his mouth. Fighting to conjure some level of self-confidence, he attempted to fight off the tightness in his chest, the numbness in his arms. His nervous system was attacking him. He flashed to his adolescence. To boys laughing at his generic sneakers. To girls mocking his eyeglasses. To ink blot drawings. To psychiatrists. And then to the mirror on Claire's wall. He had ten years and eighty pounds on her, and he was feeling every bit of them at that moment.

What happened to exile?

He was breaking his rules. He was only to share food.

Could he even remember what it meant to share something more than that?

There is not enough sensitivity in the world
There are too many things to explain

When Claire turned back to John a soft electronic beat filled the previously empty space. He recognized a Matthew Sweet song from a decade ago. It filled the air between them warmly, and helped him break momentarily from his cloud.

"Can you guess what's for dinner?" Claire asked him, looking up at his eyes. She was closer to him now that she had been.

"Fish," John replied, sniffing the air, "and something with vinegar."

"You're no fun," Claire said, slapping his nose playfully. "You know too much."

John took a step back and reached for the wine to refill her glass and his. "You'd be surprised," John answered. "This is the first time I've been out in I don't know how long."

"What do you do when the restaurant is closed?"

"Errands mostly...I watch *Law and Order*. I go to the bank. I scrub the grease filters. It's very unglamorous."

Claire moved closely in front on John. There were just a few inches between them. She wore fitted black jeans and a white blouse with a floral print. It framed her figure alluringly. "Well, tonight I'm going to add some glamor to your life." Claire said, taking a long, slow sip of wine. She clinked his glass and propped one of her bare feet on his shoe. She had purple toenails. "I've baked some salmon. I really hope you like it."

"I'm sure I will."

John listened to the expanded refrain of the song, now reaching its predictable three-minute conclusion. He smiled at Claire. "I remember a question a professor once asked our class. When a song makes you feel romantic, where does the emotion lie? Is it in the singer? Is it in the song? Or is it in the listener?"

At that minute, John was entranced by Claire, who touched his chest with her open hand. She had reached out and rested it there, over his shirt, just beside his heart, looking up at him. Her hand was warm and small. Her lips were just slightly parted. He realized they were touching for the first time since she had kissed him at *De Terre*. They were embracing. It had happened without him knowing. She had cut through his defenses.

As Claire looked up at Diver, she heard the distant voice of her father. *If you see something you want, go get it...*

Claire carefully put down her glass and pulled tightly on John's waist.

"I'm going to kiss you now, John Diver."

Fourteen

Lanny was still fairly amped as he keyed himself into his two bedroom apartment. It was not unusual for him to need an hour or two to calm himself after work. The pace of waiting tables was brisk. Yet, he had somehow grown to love it. It was in his blood. He hung his jacket on the coat rack by the door and proceeded to the kitchen, where he poured himself a generous glass of red wine.

It had been corked a few days ago, and was a bit more flat than he would have preferred, but was still wet and tart, like many of the fresher summer vintages Lanny enjoyed. He swallowed two large mouthfuls, stretched his neck and expelled a deep breath.

On the counter, his cat, Mira, sang her feline demands at him. He rubbed its thickly furred neck and reached for a treat in the cabinet. Lanny smiled at he watched Mira chew delicately. An adopted stray now three years old, the tabby was a welcome presence in Lanny's private world. His apartment had had few visitors in the past several years. It had not been intended, but neither was it unwelcome.

There had been a few dates for sure. A well-groomed actor in the local theater group had spent the night on several occasions. Their relationship was comfortable and intellectually fulfilling, but not long-lasting. Lanny continued to support the troupe as a patron and member, and enjoyed a continued friendship with his former paramour. It was one of several cultural endeavors he supported, which also included the university symphony and a regional newspaper covering ecological issues. They frequently intersected at *De Terre*, one of the de facto hubs of culture in their sleepy but progressive town.

In fact, Lanny lamented for several months the potential loss of his social base upon leaving *De Terre*. The Family Kitchen's clientele would be comprised of children and parents almost exclusively, and would surely be less cosmopolitan than his current associates. This initial fear, however, led Lanny to an important realization — one that drove him steadfast each day to his new enterprise with increasing dedication and energy. Lanny has discovered in himself an unmet paternal drive. Not so strong as to raise children himself — he understood that distinction with great clarity — but rather he had a general concern to become a mentor. The Family Kitchen would be a place for families to grow together, to renew values and to share traditions. It would be a place where the act of cooking was a bridge to a more expansive learning experience — one that included geography and math and languages. And if The Family Kitchen were a school, Lanny would be its teacher.

He had found his calling.

Lanny refilled his wine glass a second time and walked to the living room; Mira following close behind. He slouched down into his sofa and put his feet up on the ottoman. This welcome realization had transformed him. Lanny dedicated himself to the pursuit of his business with methodical rigor. Piled in stacks on the nearby coffee table were his research books. There were several glossy hardbound cookbooks by Nigella Lawson. *7 Steps to Emotional Intelligence. Teach Like Your Hair's on Fire.* A subscription to Fast Company Magazine. Other (less relevant) reading materials lay about, a few New Yorker's, a recent copy of

The Advocate. Lanny's living room had become a library. His apartment had become an office.

Consumed by his dream, Lanny found himself reinvigorated with independence. Confidence replaced insecurity. Self-love replaced his need for an affair. He had not entertained in months — and had not missed it. Rather, he appreciated the time to focus. He meditated on the immeasurables. What qualified him to be a mentor? Was it patience? Insight? Wisdom? He looked up at the framed print of a Caillebotte painting hanging on his wall. It was a café scene, pained with dexterous colorful strokes. He had bought it at the Art Institute of Chicago, falling in love with it for the quirky little dog painted in the left corner of the scene. It seemed the sum of all things. A family. A café. The sunshine. Paris. The image was perfectly self-contained.

When he was a teenager, Lanny spent much of his time on his uncle's farm. His father and his uncle were very close. They were brothers born only one year apart. They drank heavily most afternoons in the garage, collecting massive quantities of empty Genesee bottles that Lanny and his friends would redeem for movie money on weekends. The men would argue amiably over whether the Chevy or the Dodge was the better automobile. They would change the oil in their pickups, using the spent crude to paint fence posts before planting them in the yard. Most of their spare time was consumed by the 1952 Farmall Super C tractor. Each winter it was rebuilt. Each summer it exhausted itself, needing constant engine surgery to maintain the arrhythmic chortle of its 20=horsepower engine. Lanny's uncle taught him to drive the Farmall. He drove that rusted red behemoth long before he ever drove a car. Its nonsynchronous gears were stubborn but efficient.

Each summer, Lanny towed the Vermeer baler that swept across the fields leaving beautiful round hay sculptures that decorated the acreage like a scruffy minimalist installation. The first cut occurred in June, just after school ended for the summer. When the fields were cleared, great swarms of turkey buzzards would descend from the sky.

"They're eating the snakes," his uncle would say. His uncle always drove the sickle mower. He never allowed Lanny on it. Lanny had always assumed it was because it was new, a bright green John Deere. At the time it might have cost more than the farm's mortgage. Lanny was always jealous of the ease with which its silky smooth clutch engaged its twelve-speed transmission (nine forward, three reverse) with independent PTO. By comparison, driving the Farmall was more like a wrestling match.

It was only after his sixteenth birthday that Lanny realized that each cutting with the sickle mower was a slaughter. That's what drew the buzzards. The mower cut indiscriminately, brutally. His uncle dutifully captained it, a killing machine that would inevitably slice and mortally wound with its sharp rotating blades the many snakes, voles and gophers that called the fields home. In doing so he spared Lanny the killing. It was a protective act. Childless himself, Lanny's uncle treated him like his own son, wishing to keep blood off his hands for as long as possible.

Lanny was reminded of Diver's answer to the question he asked several years ago.

"Why vegetarian?" Lanny asked at the end of his job interview.

"Because there's too much death in the world," Diver responded.

That was it—love meant keeping death at bay.

Lanny believed in the power of positive energy. He believed that if he pressed all his energies into his goal, he could not fail. The Family Kitchen could not fail. It was all coming together. It was all meant to be.

After he finished his second glass, Lanny scratched at Mira's belly and smiled. He then stood up and collected the small pile of mail left on the floor below the mail slot beside the front door. Strangely, he had not thought of it before. Leafing through the unsolicited shopping ads and junk mail, his hands froze on the envelope marked with his bank's address in the upper left-hand corner.

Fifteen

John felt Claire's lips softly meet his, recoil, then meet again. Her mouth opened, and her moist tongue touched his timidly at first, and then deeply as she moaned almost imperceptibly. Diver tasted hot salt and mint, and cupped the side of her face in his hand as he returned her passion. Her arms tightened around his lower waist, and she dug several fingers beneath his belt to the small of his back.

They stopped for a moment, taking deep breaths and changing the sides of their embrace before kissing deeply again, this time plunging intensely into each other's mouths. Their embrace lasted hours, or perhaps minutes. Time was forced still.

As they paused for a moment, Claire opened her eyes and looked sheepishly up to John. "I guess we broke the ice," she cooed in his ear.

John found himself chuckling. His heart raced. "Technically, I think you did, Claire."

"I've wanted to do that for a long time."

"I don't know why."

"I do."

"I think your salmon's burning."

"I don't care."

As if being controlled by an outside force, John suddenly picked Claire up and sat her on the hutch against the wall. A picture frame fell. She didn't react. His hand reached through her hair and brought her head to his. As he kissed her madly, she wrapped her legs around his waist and pulled herself into him, feeling the swelling beneath his pants. She, too, had become aware of her own arousal, and Diver's aggression accelerated it. It was something she hadn't expected, and she found it most welcome.

Dinner would come later. Right now, they were hungry for each other.

A moment later, Claire pulled herself away from John. She put her hand over his lips. "Wait," she said with heavy breath.

In that instant Diver waited for the cameras to come out of their hiding, for the host to pronounce the ruse to the audience. He wanted to turn and run, but could only freeze. His face reddened. He waited for the show lights to come up. For the music to play.

Claire pushed him gently away and walked to the kitchen. She said nothing. She smiled at Diver in the pass-through and turned off the oven. She then shut the light switch and blew out the candles on the table. She pulled the scrunchy from her curly hair and let it fall as she shook her head. She grabbed John's hand. Pulling it to her lips, she kissed one of his fingers, sucking just slightly at its tip. She giggled nervously. Taking his hand in hers, she then walked him towards her bedroom.

"I just didn't want a fire," she said, rubbing her body against his as they moved.

Diver entered the bedroom like an explorer in the wilderness. He had little precedent for the experience before him. He was alarmed and invigorated, incredulous and grateful. Claire motioned for him to sit on the edge of her bed, a pillow-top twin with a quilt that was perfectly clean and scented with apple. A Courbet print hung on the wall, as did a photograph of a man and a woman, presumably her parents, who looked down at him. There was an oak wardrobe and a bright yellow beanbag chair. Claire walked to the far wall and lowered the lights, which were on a dimmer, so that the room fell to shadow. She then moved directly in front of Diver, who sat on the bed looking up at her.

Claire slowly unbuttoned her blouse, looking down at John, saying nothing. Her eyes met his with intensity. She let the blouse fall behind her, and then unclasped her bra from the front. Letting it go, she reached for John's hand and stood him up, placing his hand on her breast, which she then covered with hers. When he grasped her, she exhaled into his mouth. Her breath was hot.

John looked down at the gold choker Claire always wore, at the thin line of her collarbone, and at her breasts, which rose from her freckled chest. He hastily unbuttoned his own shirt, letting it fall, and touched her bare torso with his. He was enlivened by her youth, by her frailty, by the paleness of her skin.

Claire heated with the touch of his chest, which was almost hairless, on hers. She stretched up on her toes and pecked Diver's lips repeatedly, almost like a child, as she unbuckled his belt and loosened his pants. They fell to the floor. She lightly brushed the hard flesh between his legs, and pulled his boxers down below his knees. She felt him unbuttoning her jeans, and she shuffled out of her fitted denim. She helped John take her boyshorts to the floor. Claire felt John between her thighs, and she lifted one leg around his back to intensify the pressure.

Losing their balance, they fell over onto the bed, Claire landing on top of John. She lifted herself up to offer him a view of her exposed body. She was no longer nervous. She wanted Diver to see all she wanted to give to him, all that she wanted to be his.

She was surprised to see a large tattoo on his chest, a glyph of some kind, looking like an abstract figure. She found it exciting, to imagine the pain it must have caused him, and to imagine that it could be the secret they kept between them. She leaned down and kissed the tattoo. She lightly pinched his nipple with her lips. John groaned. This was her moment now. She positioned her wet pelvis over his, knees pressed out at his sides. With her hand she glided him inside her and felt him fill her. She knew he wouldn't be long. She didn't care. She had everything she wanted.

Sixteen

John woke in the dim light of dawn, as it splintered in sharp patterns over the closed blinds of Claire's window. She was nestled under his arm, which was somewhat numb from its position. The day was quiet. The day was striking, in its infancy, surrounding them. He looked down at Claire's sleeping face. Her freckles were coming to life in the morning light. Her hair was thickened and straightened from all the times John ran his hand through it.

What could this lovely girl want with him? It had been so long since he had considered romance possible. Decades, in fact, since the last time he felt the slightest pulse of carnal vitality. Outside of a few drunken kisses with a lovely and troubled Italian waitress there was only a high school love, a talented burgeoning pianist, who had ever really haunted his desires. As much as he wanted her, he ultimately terrified her with his dark moods and drug use. She confided in him after their graduation that she needed to hurt him in order to not hurt herself. She thought he was broken, and for so long he accepted she was right.

As if to counter that belief, Claire itched her nose and began to blink her eyes open. She smiled up at John's face. "Good morning," she whispered.

"Good morning," John replied smiling.

She looked at him and laughed sheepishly. "Our date seemed to go pretty well."

"I had imagined it differently."

"Oh, yeah?" Claire asked, "How differently?'

"Well, I figured I'd start by saying something foolish."

"I guess it's a good thing I didn't give you much time to talk," she giggled.

"I guess so."

Claire raised herself with her elbow, allowing John to move his arm from beneath her head. She looked at him from the side.

John was unnerved at how she looked at him. Not differently now, but rather the same way she always had. She locked on his eyes. She penetrated them, staring more deeply than most, more intimately than most. She was attentive, focused, alluring. John had never looked at another human being like that in his life. He secretly hoped she had not either.

Was this how Aschenbach saw Venice? As if each moment contained a multitude of presents and futures, each cascading with life's raw energy and potential? Is it life itself that can suddenly explode within a man? Or is it the man who must decipher life first? And what if it is too late? Can it be too late?

The moment in front of Diver seemed endless.

Claire's gaze was targeted. She said nothing, though expressed to him openness and sincerity. She did not seem to care about time. She could speak again in seconds or in hours. It did not matter.

John looked into her eyes, which were pools of a light-brown hue. They did not move but in blinking, which occurred in rhythm. John knew there was something to those eyes. They bore joy and sadness equally. Subtly, almost imperceptibly, they betrayed her resolution. Within her iris, a translucent spark of amber occasionally caught light. Diver found himself defenseless. How had he never seen those eyes before? They were not garish. She wore only liner to highlight their contour. They were not hidden. Her hair hung in bangs just the edge of her brows.

They had been there for him to see all along.

Without forethought, John moved to her and kissed her. His lips were dry. Claire's were wet.

"It's about time," Claire smiled.

John ran his hand through her bangs. "Do you have school today?"

"Later," Claire said, now kissing him. "Right now I have you."

In such moments, there is little else to say. Diver wanted her again. Claire wanted him. As he moved onto her, and then into her, the sun broke through the window and brightened the room. She moaned in his ear. He felt himself losing control.

Three hours later, Diver keyed the lock of *De Terre*. For the first time since its opening, he wished he were somewhere else.

Seventeen

Lanny dried his eyes in front of the mirror. They were pink and bulbous. He had not slept well, even after opening a second bottle of wine. The destruction of one's dream is funny that way — it kills one's present and one's future in the same cleave. His bank had declined his loan. Mark had been transferred. It was all a terrible surprise. At least to Lanny.

I'm sorry, Mr. Sabatelli, but Mr. Stofner has left for the Philadelphia office. Our other loan officers are absorbing his accounts. We hope to help you in future endeavors...

It was bullshit dreck from a bullshit office drone. Late the night before, one bottle of wine in, Lanny drove down to Blair Street, hoping to throw at least one brick through the window of the former internet cafe, only to find a SOLD sign proudly displayed on its sidewalk. Lanny had been shunned, it seemed, for another applicant. Instead of rage, Lanny could muster only submission. He was done. The Family Kitchen was done. Soon the building would be a Kinkos, or a Subway, or an OTB. It didn't matter. The system wanted what it wanted, and the people would take it up the ass.

Lanny returned home. Breaking glass would not change the situation. He opened another bottle of wine and drank on his couch, Mira on his lap, knowing he was powerless. It was folly to dream. American was no longer a place for dreamers.

Several hours later, after a restless sleep and long hot shower, Lanny attempted to shake it all off. After all, he had to work that afternoon, in the one place where he felt most comfortable. The one place he felt like he mattered. There would be customers, but they would be the easy part. If they knew him at all they knew him only superficially. Even the reading group was not fully aware of his venture. The real difficulty lied in seeing John. Lanny could not keep his failure from him. Surely he would break down in some wretched display of emotion, laying bare his distress in front of the man in his life he most admired. Lanny could not know that he was John's beacon of hope — that he was the compass by which John navigated his world. No, Lanny could only presume he would be diminished in John's eyes. And so, as in the past, he would come to personify failure amongst those closest to him.

At least he would do so in his nicest shirt.

As he donned his Marcella wing collar, he breathed deeply. He was a professional. He had a job to do, even with a throbbing head. The bastards could not take that from him.

One hour after, he walked through the front door of *De Terre*. It could have been any day in the last two years, but it was not.

"Hi, Chef," he chirped, seeing John behind the bar. It was unusual for him to be in the front of the house.

"Lanny, my friend," Diver replied, pouring a ginger ale from the soda gun. John seemed more social than usual.

"What's up?" Lanny queried. He squinted like a detective. "You look different."

John was momentarily caught off guard. "Well, I'm recently showered," he responded heartily.

"Well, I appreciate your hygiene," Lanny retorted, then paused to take the situation in, "but that's not it. You're actually smiling today."

"I don't smile?"

"No. Not really."

"Perhaps I'm just happy to see you, Lanny."

"No. That's not it either."

John scratched his head. "But I am happy to see you. I'm always happy to see you."

"Yes, well, something's going on. Something different. I'll figure it out."

John laughed. "No more interrogations until after the dinner rush. I've got all these potatoes to deal with."

"You can't hide from me, Chef," Lanny followed, swallowing the irony willingly.

"I brought out the fruit for your prep, " John replied. With that he pushed through the swinging door of the kitchen. Lanny sighed, paused for a few seconds, and took out the small polypropylene cutting board behind the bar and positioned it to cut lemons and limes for the evening. After the first slice, it hit him. He looked back to the kitchen. He smiled, happy to concentrate on something other than his failure. He left the fruit momentarily, and found a piece of chalk by the register and scribed

JD

+

CD

on the wall of truth. It looked good next to the other graffiti. He would wait to see if anyone noticed it.

Back in the kitchen, John boiled potatoes while listening to the hockey talk on the radio. The Rangers, with their new coach, were looking at the playoffs. He listened casually as organized his line. The evening's special would be potato enchiladas, from a recipe a friend from Tijuana gave him many years ago. In front of him was a large steel bowl of tomatillos, which he dehusked and halved with his Hoffritz quickly. He dropped the fruit into a pot holding two cups of simmering vegetable stock, along with several cloves of roasted caramelized garlic. As the tomatillos broke down he added just a pinch of baking soda to reduce the acid. The sauce foamed, releasing gas, for a few seconds. He added a small mirepoix of finely diced carrots and red onions with a half-teaspoon of epazote. Looking over at his potatoes, their red skins now peeling back from the white flesh within, he turned off the flame and reached for a towel. Grabbing the long aluminum handle with it, Diver quickly dumped the tubers into a colander over his prep sink, the steam rising and temporarily fogging his glasses. He left the potatoes and took the pot of tomatillos off the heat to cool slightly.

The musical intro to the Blueshirts pregame had him turning suddenly to watch. Rolling his sleeves up, he glanced up at the clock and lit the steam table to prepare his station for dinner. Dinnertime had almost arrived. Even though it was early winter, the townies were still sitting down to eat on the late side, as they did in the summer. February started to bring around the five o'clock tables. Turning back to his line, he procured a ball of dough from the reach-in and laid it on parchment to roll out. Despite spending every moment thinking about Claire, John's timing remained precise.

Walking to his food processor with the tomatillos, John carefully ladled the still-hot sauce in, blending it on low speed to a slightly thickened puree. He reserved the sauce in a one-sixth pan following a final flourish of sea salt and white pepper. The potatoes were next up, in this case, mashed by hand with some milk, butter, fresh roasted corn, black pepper, salt and a chiffonade of flat-leaf parsley. He tasted the mix to his satisfaction. Freshly made corn tortillas and farmers cheese would complete the entrée, along with black bean soup and grilled chayote squash. He made a plate for Lanny, and then turned to his quiche.

For Diver, quiche was now synonymous with Claire. He wanted it perfect, so that every mouthful could dance on her tongue and remind her of him. He imagined that his food was a greater seducer than he, and perhaps the reason she was so incomprehensibly attracted to him in the first place. After all, it certainly wasn't his chiseled body, his dark features, slim waistline or rugged appeal. He could only imagine her coming to her senses soon enough, when a too bright light exposed his belly, or the mole on his back, or the hair in his ear. When enough of her friends teased her. When Facebook unfriended her. Diver knew she would come to her senses soon enough, but not before he ravished her taste buds like no other man could.

Taking a firm grasp of his marble rolling pin, he rolled the cool dough on the parchment to create a circle. Flipping it over into his favorite skillet, he tucked the sides and cut the excess away with his paring knife. With a pastry brush, he painted the dough with clarified butter and ground fresh pepper lightly. After dotting holes at the base with a fork and checking for consistency, he spread some Parmesan cheese over the base and popped the dough into the oven for ten minutes.

Diver entered his walk-in to gather ingredients for the filling. In a steel bowl he placed some portabellas, porcinis, fresh chives, cream cheese and topped it with a flat of eggs. After walking them over to his cutting board, he coarsely diced the mushroom duo. He placed sixteen ounces of cream cheese at the end of his salamander to warm in the package. Dicing the chives finely, he reserved them in a nearby soup cup. In a heavy-bottomed sauté pan, he heated some truffle oil and added the mushrooms. They sizzled softly, absorbing rich flavor, wilting slightly over the heat. Diver watched as they shrank, deglazing them with two ounces of sherry. He then returned the mixture to the bowl to cool.

He quickly separated four eggs, adding the whites to a copper bowl. With a whisk he proficiently beat them to soft peaks. To the mushrooms, he added twelve eggs and the four yolks, some cream, pink salt and the softened cream cheese. These he gently heated in a double boiler on the stovetop. After warming the custard he folded in the whites, and the volume of the mix expanded. Turing around to the stove, he pulled the great skillet from the oven and carefully poured the batter into the golden crust, topping it with the chives and a drizzle of oil. It was done.

It was four-fifty.

As he looked up at the clock, John noticed the hockey talk had gone to static, so he adjusted the radio knob to retrace the station. He crossed over into a conservative talk line, which was lit up over a Robert Mapplethorpe exhibition. Not THE Robert Mapplethorpe exhibition. This one was based on his floral photographs. But evidently, people were angered just the same.

What the angry callers couldn't know was that they had already won. Well not they, specifically, but the market, which won on their behalf. Big business was in charge now. The writing seemed to be on the wall. Just that month Benjamin Buchloh had argued the avant-garde extinct, or at least, co-opted, having been officially stamped and endorsed by the market. He smartly recognized that the market moved more quickly than artists, commodifying counterculture for its own agenda, alluring the artist to it with high dollar sales. He stated:

Artists have been increasingly integrated into an ever-expanding structure of cultural control by mirroring in their work the apparatus of industrialized culture itself.

With Mapplethorpe gone, there were few to take his place. People were angry for no reason. They were yelling at a ghost. It would be capitalism itself that created the next ideological rift in their worldview, if the rift were even recognizable to them. It would certainly be packaged well. It would probably be sold in Walmart.

As he turned the knob back to his sports station, John was thankful for the open-mindedness of his town, however moderate it was. It was no Amsterdam, but the small liberal arts university provided the farming community two things, social activities and a multicultural populace. Exposure to difference made all the difference. There were still lines firmly drawn of course, which John knew all too well through his friendship with Lanny, but *De Terre* was an example of how people were more alike than disparate, at least when it came to the stomach.

Perhaps that was it. While it seemed implausible, perhaps he and Claire were more alike than different. They were both well-read. Both appreciated knowledge. Both liked good food. Could it be enough?

Time would tell. The clock had started last night.

Just then, Lanny pushed through the door to the kitchen with a small notepad.

"John, we have nine reservations tonight. All deuces. Starting at six."

"Great. Are we open?"

"I thought I'd unlock at 5:15, unless I see someone."

"Sounds good. Here," he said, offering an enchilada plate, "I made a special for you. Red potato enchiladas. It's not too spicy."

Lanny looked at the plate and picked up a nearby fork. "It looks good. Is this cactus?"

"Squash," Diver replied. "It's got a great texture. Mild flavor. It will go great with that Moscato you ordered."

Lanny responded with a mouthful. "Mmm. This is nice, John. I didn't know how hungry I was." He continued to eat in great bites, feeling the sweat of his hangover still clinging slightly to his head and chest. He had not eaten since the night before.

"Also, soup tonight is red lentil. And the quiche is wild mushroom with cream cheese. I also have two orders of manicotti left from yesterday."

Lanny swallowed. "Any new desserts?"

"I made a banana cake that will go out with ganache. And I have apples with warm caramel. Oh, and I got some blueberries in. I'm making a sorbet tomorrow, but if anyone wants a bowl tonight, I can whip up some cream to go with them."

As Lanny scraped up the last of the tomatillo sauce, he met John eyes. Fork in his mouth, he need every ounce of his willpower to keep from bursting into tears. He swallowed his emotion. Then, one moment later, the feeling was gone, as if it never happened.

John looked at him quizzically. "Are you OK, Lanny?"

Lanny feigned vigor. "Oh, yes, fine," he said, "A little too much wine last night. I should have just eaten more slowly."

"Well, it's Friday," John replied, "I wouldn't notice if you had a little hair of the dog before we open."

Lanny smiled briefly and looked down at the floor. It wasn't a bad idea.

"That's not a bad idea."

He bussed his plate and turned to leave the kitchen. "Thanks, John," he said, avoiding direct eye contact. He then checked his notepad again. "Oh, yes, we do have one three-top at seven. Simon, Liz, and your new girlfriend."

With that, he left, the door swinging shut before John could even look up from his cutting board in surprise.

Eighteen

"I don't know. Maybe I'm an old soul or something. I'm sick of men my age." Liz was aware of hogging the conversation, but she needed to let off a little steam after a tense week at school.

Claire responded supportingly, "You deserve better than Alex, Liz. He's a child."

"It's like I have this sign on me that says, 'Mature men need not apply' or something. I ask you, where have all the Simons gone?

Long time passing…

They both sang together, laughing.

Liz was carefully piloting her Toyota Camry down the curving hill into town. The first major snowfall of the season was in progress, dusting the roads with a light sheen of white powder. It was not yet enough for the plows, but more was on its way. She and Claire were on their way to *De Terre*, looking forward to a good meal together.

"You know, he says he's interested in me. So I cover his class on Wednesday so he could go to that conference in the city.

And when he gets back, he says he didn't think we were in a relationship."

"Ass!"

"Well," Liz continued, "that's the last time I go down on a guy on the first date."

Claire laughed. "No, it's not."

Liz laughed harder. "You're right."

As she hugged the last turn before the road straightened, Liz turned up the volume of her radio. "Have you heard this, Claire? It's the new Radiohead."

"Yeah," Claire answered, "it's pretty good."

"You want to go dancing after dinner?"

"Where, at the Hub? No, thanks. I like the way my clothes smell."

"C'mon, I need a wingman."

"No, you don't. Besides, you just said you were sick of men your age."

"Damn. I hate it when you're right. Let's change the subject. What's up with your chef? You've been dallying for weeks. Are you going to bang that old man or what?"

"He's thirty-six," Claire retorted. "He's hardly old."

Liz glanced at Claire impishly. "I noticed you quibbled with the "old" part and not the "bang" part."

Claire looked out the passenger side window. She did not respond.

Liz's eyes widened. "Holy crap!"

"What?"

"Holy crap!"

Claire could not maintain her face. She felt her cheeks reddening.

"You slept with him, didn't you? That's why you didn't call me back the other night. You were banging the chef."

"Liz…"

"You were sampling his sausage."

"If you'll calm down, I'll tell you what happened.'

"Did you use utensils?"

"That doesn't even make sense. Are you done now? Can we have a normal conversation?"

"Yes. I'm done. Now tell me EVERTHING."

With that, Liz pulled in the *De Terre* parking lot. Small as it was, it never seemed to be full. She shut off the engine, keeping the radio and interior light on. Unlocking her safety belt, she turned to Claire and hugged her with great affection. "I'm so happy for you. Tell me everything."

Claire released her safety belt and put her hand on Liz's knee. She turned the radio down slightly and took a breath. "Well, you remember last week after dinner? You walked over to the bar with Simon. Well, long story short, John and I were talking. And I'm not sure if it was the wine or what, but I kissed him."

Liz looked incredulous. "You didn't tell me that? You drove me home!"

"It was quick, and on the cheek. It was a lunge really. Besides, I was worried I had made a mistake."

"And?"

"We went on a date last night. Not an official date, I guess. I offered to cook for him. You know, because he always cooks for me.

"And?"

"He came to my apartment. We had some wine."

"And?"

Claire was sure her face was now completely red. Luckily, the car was dark. "And I jumped him. We didn't even get to eat dinner. He spent the night, and we woke up together this morning."

"Holy crap. I love you. You're my hero."

Claire smiled warmly. "Now I need you to be on your best behavior, Liz. I like this guy. Don't bust his chops when we get in there."

"I won't. I swear. I'm so happy for you. But just wait two more minutes. I need more details."

"Well, if you must know, I found myself with an opening." Claire began retelling the story, suddenly enjoying her role. "We were standing outside the kitchen, waiting on the salmon to be done. It was weird. I got really brash for a moment. I told him I was going to kiss him. Before I knew it, he had picked me up and, bam, I had my legs around his waist."

"Get out!"

"It was pretty intense," Claire answered. "I mean, it was quick, but it was intense."

"Let me repeat. You are my hero."

"And this morning. It was just as intense…"

"And?" Liz goaded.

"And not as quick."

"Good girl," Liz exclaimed happily. "All right, I'm going to let you off the hook for now because I'm going to be a proper lady. But later I want measurements, graphic details and video recordings if you have them. With footnotes if possible."

As they left the vehicle together, Liz reached over and put her arm around Claire. Walking in tandem, they meandered from the parking lot to the restaurant sidewalk.

"Maybe I'll go home with Simon," Liz whispered. "Then we can both get some tonight. If only he was forty years younger."

"Or you were forty years older."

"Don't ever say that again," Liz quipped, opening the door to *De Terre*.

As they walked in, Lanny met their eyes and waived to them. After hanging their jackets, they proceeded to a table where Simon awaited them, sipping a cocktail. He rose as they both sat, and then reclaimed his seat, bidding them hello in a warm casual voice. Claire looked around the room, seeing three tables of couples in various stages of eating. She recognized one woman from the university library, who was a staff member there, and very helpful to her on one occasion. Everyone seemed to be on a date.

To their left the fireplace crackled softly. The room was comfortable and quiet, stirring only with the occasional clink of glasses and plateware.

"How are you tonight, Simon?"

"I'm good, Claire. Thank you. And how are the both of you?"

"Good," Claire answered.

"Excellent, Simon," said Liz. "You look very handsome tonight."

Simon chuckled. "It's not every day a man of my age has dinner with two elegant young women. I imagine I am the envy of every man in this room."

At that moment, Lanny appeared at the table to greet them.

"Good evening, ladies. How are we tonight? Will we be having cocktails or a bottle of wine with dinner?"

"I'd like that pinot again, Lanny."

"The Wallace Brook."

"Let's do a bottle," Claire interjected.

"A bottle of Wallace Brook coming up. And I'll return with today's menu in just a moment." With that, Lanny turned and walked to the bar.

Claire whispered to Liz. "Do you recognize that woman over there?"

Liz turned subtly and replied. "No I don't. Do you?'

"I'm pretty sure she's a librarian."

Simon stirred his drink with a small straw. "How are things at the university?"

Liz answered first. "I lost at love, Simon. And worse yet, with a classmate."

"I'm sorry, Dear," he comforted, and then dryly replied, "Is this man brain-dead?"

They laughed together. Simon had a way of breaking the ice.

"I finished a big part of my thesis research," Claire offered. "I'm kind of celebrating."

Liz lit up. "That's not why you're celebrating!"

Lanny returned to the table with the wine, corked it, and poured a taste in Liz's glass. She sampled it and nodded. Lanny poured two glasses for the women and set the bottle on the table along with the cork.

"Shall I give you some time to relax, or would you like to look at the menu?"

Simon replied. "A few moments, Lanny, thank you. I'd like my date to last as long as possible."

"Of course," Lanny said, then looking down at his seven and seven. "Would you like another drink?"

"Thank you, yes."

As Claire and Liz each sipped a first taste of the pinot, Simon returned to the conversation. "What research did you complete, Claire?"

"I've been researching a one-armed privateer named Captain John MacPherson. He pirated French ships during the Seven Years War. After, he tried to buy himself into various circles of Philadelphia-based revolutionaries. Toward the end of his life, he self-published his autobiography. So I've been attempting to corroborate some of his claims through the Philadelphia Museum, which has a few of his original letters."

"Fascinating," Simon responded. "A one-armed privateer turned revolutionary."

Claire kept going. "It gets better. He was also an amateur astronomer and scientist. And had dinner with John Adams."

"And you're going to bring him to life again?"

"Maybe. I'd like to."

"Sing the songs of men and they will never die."

Liz followed, "Don't forget women."

Simon smiled, "Tonight, let us drink to women and to one-armed men." They sipped their glasses together. At that moment, Lanny came from the kitchen with two plates for the table across the room. The motion caught all their eyes. After a pause, Simon leaned into the table and looked at Claire.

"I've never seen John happier, Dear, and I feel that you are the reason for it."

Claire blushed. She had been caught by surprise.

"I arrived just a small time before you, but it was enough for me to say hello to him," Simon continued. "Something seemed different about him, but it wasn't until Lanny told me that I knew."

Liz interrupted. "Seriously, am I the last to know everything here?

At that moment, Lanny came back to the table with Simon's fresh cocktail. "Don't blame me, Liz. I've only known for an hour."

"Then I guess we're tied," she replied.

"Would you like me to come back in five for your order? Let you chat a bit?"

"Thanks, Lanny, that would be perfect," Liz answered. "And see if you can do some more recon for us."

Lanny laughed and walked to the next table.

Claire finally had the chance to respond to Simon. "We had a date," she said with a smile. "It was a good one."

"Lovely to know," Simon added.

"Yeah," Liz injected, "good seems to be an understatement from the story I heard."

"Liz! You promised to be on your best behavior."

"And I will be. I'm just jealous."

"We all find love in due time, Dear," Simon said. "Even our one-armed pirate, I suspect?"

Claire smiled. "Yes, he was married twice. But the first ended very badly."

"Was he married with or without the arm?" Liz queried.

"One with and one without, I think." Claire answered, then shrugging to her company. "I'll find more out when I go to D.C. next week. I'll be snooping around the Library of Congress."

"I wish I were going with you," Liz said. "I love going to the Smithsonian. My parents took us there every summer."

"Tell me about it," Simon inquired.

Liz took a sip of wine and replied. "I remember the first time I saw my dad cry was in front of the Star-Spangled Banner. We waited in line for twenty minutes. My brother had to go to the bathroom. He was too young to care. It is housed in this half-circular amphitheater type of thing and when you turn a corner, bam! There it is. The first thing you notice is how big it is, and the second is how quiet everyone becomes. It's in tatters really, but somehow so perfect in its condition. It always made me proud to see it. I don't really know why. It's like it was just a part of me, and a part of everyone else around you. I went each summer for five years. My dad called it the best piece of modern art in the world."

At that point, Lanny wandered over to the table and filled each of the wine glasses from the bottle. He noted Simon's glass, which did not yet need refreshing. "How are we folks? Shall I take your orders?"

"Perfect timing," Claire approved. "You know what I'll have."

"One quiche, room temperature. This evening's is mushroom with lavender cream cheese."

Liz peered over the menu. "Hmm, what do I want, Lanny?"

"If you're asking me, I'd say the soup and the penne."

"Mmm. The soup, yes. Not the pasta. Something lighter...I'll have the warm spinach salad."

Lanny bowed. "Soup and salad for the lady. And for the gentleman?"

"I will have the soup and the quiche, Lanny."

Claire interjected. "I think I'll start with the soup, too, Lanny."

"Wonderful," Lanny replied, "Anything else?"

Liz smiled. "You might as well open another bottle for us when you have the chance. We're celebrating."

"What's the occasion?"

"The official story is Claire's thesis."

"Congratulations, Claire," Lanny returned. "Is it complete?"

Claire shook her head and swallowed. "Oh, no. I've still got four months. But I had a major breakthrough."

"Two major breakthroughs." Liz added.

As Claire elbowed Liz, Lanny raised his brows and smirked, knowing exactly what Liz had meant.

Upon entering the kitchen he exclaimed to John, "Order up, Chef. Three soups. Two quiche and a spinach salad for our guests. Did you know Claire was celebrating her thesis breakthrough?"

"Actually, I didn't," John answered sheepishly. "Is it finished?"

"No, but apparently it will be in May."

That reality punched John in the face. May. Mere months away. He tried to look unshaken. But after a pause he looked up to find that Lanny, too, had his head down across the line.

After a pregnant moment, Lanny looked up to him. "Take my advice, John. Don't blow this. Don't let life pass you by."

Nineteen

"The iron Buddha cannot cross the furnace." Liz said to the group.

"What does that mean?" Jacob asked.

"It's a Zen saying. It means that one philosophy can never be right for every situation."

The group was reading Camus' *The Plague* at Liz's request. The book had generated a conversation surrounding irrationality in life.

"That's what Camus was saying. Father Paneloux represents dogma. And dogma dies." Bill dominated the conversation as usual, gesturing with his hands as he spoke.

Claire answered, "But neither was he saying that nothing mattered. Tarrou proves that."

"Well said, my dear," Simon added. "I'd like to thank you, Liz, for introducing us to this book. It's quite complex. I can't help but wonder how we would react to such a potentially dangerous situation."

At that moment, John entered the room with a tray of food. As all eyes turned to him he smiled and placed the tray down on the table.

"Hi, gang," he said. "Here's some brain food."

Before them he laid a two-pound wheel of cheese and a basket of corn muffins. A bowl of grapes and some cherry tomatoes completed the offering.

"Let me know what you think of this Havarti. I made it myself."

"Are you kidding? You make your own cheese, too?" Liz smiled.

"Sometimes. This is one of the easier ones."

Claire stole a glance at John who smiled at her sheepishly. She averted her glance in embarrassment after they made eye contact. They were like two teenagers at a high school dance.

Liz grabbed a knife and sank it into the soft cheese, revealing the fresh dill infused into its body. After popping a small cube into her mouth she purred. "Holy crap! This is fantastic."

"Liz has a way with words, John," Claire responded. "She gets right to the point."

As the group began to take some of the repast, Simon looked up to John, still standing beside the table.

"Have you read this one, John?" he asked, pointing to the book in his hand.

"No," John replied. "Good?"

"Indeed," Simon continued. "It asks all the important questions."

John smiled, "Let me guess, no answers, right?"

Simon smiled back, "Correct answers are never given. They must be deduced."

"Well said."

As John began to turn and head back to the kitchen, Claire pushed out a chair with her foot. "Stay for a bit, John. I brought a good shiraz."

John was happy for the invite and sat down beside Claire. She wore a dark-green sweater with red pants and brown boots. He noticed a bit of green eye shadow highlighting her eyes. Her lips were glossy.

Claire cut John a cube of cheese. To the surprise of the table, she placed it into his mouth by hand. "What is your expert opinion, Chef?"

John chewed and nodded his head. "Not half bad," he replied. As Claire poured him a small glass of wine he turned to Liz.

"This was your choice?" he asked, pointing to the book.

Liz swallowed a bite of her muffin. "Yes. It's the only Camus I haven't read. What better time?"

"So, what were you discussing?"

"Reason," Simon answered, "or the lack thereof."

Liz smiled. "Mostly the lack."

Simon rested back in his chair. He took a deep breath before continuing. "What governs us? Is it faith? Is it fear? Selfishness? Empathy? Greed? Camus presents us with a character that represents each of these conditions. Paneloux is faith. Tarrou is empathy. Cottard is greed."

"And Rambert is love," Liz added. "He wanted nothing more than to see his wife again."

As John sipped at his shiraz he suddenly felt Claire's hand on his thigh. Hidden from the rest of the table, the two shared a moment of intimacy.

"Each of these characters on their own could not stop the Plague," Simon continued.

Jacob was following Simon. "And that Plague could just be a metaphor for any cataclysm in which we lose control."

"Exactly," Simon continued. "It is how the characters respond to tragedy that defines them."

Bill, who remained silent while eating, jumped in. "But, Simon, there is a counter to that message. And that is that life is absurd. Camus shows us that we are powerless in the wake of forces greater than we are."

"Powerless to stop them, yes," Simon answered. "But not powerless to meet them with grace."

"Like Dr. Rieux," Claire began, siding with Pence. "Dr. Rieux is just an ordinary man in many ways. But his kindness is the best response to the epidemic. "*The Plague* isn't about the plague. Its about Rieux."

"Or, I would add, the Rieux in all of us."

Bill interjected once more. "OK, I buy that. But we must admit that it's not just the Rieux in all of us. It's the others, too. Raoul. Gonzales. The weak and the strong."

"I'd agree to that, Bill." Simon noted.

"Me, too." Liz added.

At that point John noticed the clock over the bar. "Well," he said, "it sounds like you are all close to agreement. I'm going to finish up a few things in the kitchen. I'll come back with desert in twenty minutes or so." When he rose, his thigh felt cold in the absence of Claire's touch.

As Bill continued talking Liz glanced over to Claire, who watched John enter the kitchen. She poked her in the hip and gestured that she follow him. "Go on," she whispered.

"Shhh!" Claire pursed back.

"So I read that the book may be an allegory for the German occupation," Bill spoke aloud, attempting a new conversation.

Liz poked Claire again.

"Ouch!" Claire exclaimed.

"What is the matter, Dear?" Simon asked Claire.

"Nothing, Simon," she hesitated, "Excuse me just a minute. I'm going to ask John something."

She got up and turned to the swinging door.

Simon smiled over to Liz as Claire left the table. "Are you to thank for that?'

Liz smiled back. "No. It's Camus. He taught me that time waits for no woman."

Twenty

There are five mother sauces for classical French cuisine — Concassé de tomate, Velouté, Hollandaise, Espagnole and Béchamel. Of these, two require meat; veal is used for Espagnole and chicken or fish bones for Velouté. Diver worked many months to perfect a roasted vegetable reduction that served as a staple in many of his sauces. While lighter and thinner than demi-glace, it had similar depth of flavor, both salty and savory, and rich in aromatic complexity.

It took Diver about three days to fill a five-gallon bucket with vegetable scraps. The ends of onions and carrots, celery leaves and hearts, as well as less habitual additions like mushroom stems and the outer leaves of leeks are never wasted in a proper kitchen. When filled, Diver would add these ingredients along garlic, squash, and fresh tomatoes to a three-gallon roasting pan. After tossing the mixture quickly in olive oil, he slid the uncovered pan into an oven at 375 degrees for thirty minutes.

Once this first stage of the sauce was complete, Diver opened the oven and deglazed the pan with a bottle of Chianti, allowing it to reduce for ten minutes. Next came the addition of two gallons of water, along with a generous addition of fresh herbs, juniper berries, and whole pepper. The fusion would then cook in the oven for ninety minutes, reducing the liquid by more than half, before it would be removed from heat. After cooling, it was triple strained, salted, and if necessary, further reduced on the stovetop.

De Terre was closed that evening, but a special table for two had been reserved. Diver had come in a few hours prior to make his reduction and keep himself busy so as not to obsess on the evening. He was making a potato cabbage salad with a sampling of cheeses for the meal.

After boiling ten ounces of baby red potatoes, he allowed them to cool on a clean towel to absorb excess moisture. With his Hoffritz, he cleaved a cabbage head in two and cut it quickly to leave rectangular leaves of approximately two inches in length and one inch in width. He smiled as he thought of how important the geometry of food was to a diligent chef. Size did matter. After immersing them in a boiling pot of water with a cup of fresh vegetable reduction, he halved the now cooled potatoes and wiped them into a steel bowl with his right hand. Two minutes later, he strained the cabbage from its broth and shocked it in ice water for 30 seconds before folding the leaves out onto the same towel used for the potatoes.

Glancing up at the clock above the line, Diver grabbed a small steel bowl and poured a quarter cup of olive oil into it, following with several tablespoons of malt vinegar, honey, and two tablespoons of fresh loosely cut tarragon. He then folded the towel over and wrung out any remaining water from the cabbage leaves before adding them to the potatoes. Whisking the dressing deftly, he poured the liquid into the bowl and added a tablespoon of freshly ground pepper and pink salt. With a simple toss, the zesty dish was complete.

He placed the bowl in his cooler for the moment and turned his attention to the protein. On a wooden board, he placed a few small cheeses of Dutch and French variety and a ramekin of triple-cream brie. At that moment he heard a voice from the front of the house. It was Claire. John had given her a key several days before.

"Hi, sweetheart!" she flirted as she poked her head through the swinging door. "Table for two?"

Diver's heart warmed to see her. She walked into the kitchen and kissed him playfully. "I'm hungry."

"I just finished," Diver replied. "Why don't you pick out a wine, and I'll be right out?"

As she nodded and turned back to the dining room. Diver plated two salads on seven-inch plates and set them on a serving tray with the cheeses and a baguette, along with silverware. Pushing through the swinging door, he brought the tray out into the dining room to see that Claire had brought her own candle and lit it on their table. Her face glowed in its soft light.

"Ohhh," she voiced quietly, "I feel like I'm in Europe." She picked up a small wedge of Parrano and popped it into her mouth.

John sat and sipped the wine she had poured. "In Europe, I'd be better dressed. And probably thinner, too."

"I wouldn't change a thing, John Diver."

"Have you been to Europe?" he asked, ripping some bread for them.

Claire ate a forkful of the cabbage salad. "Mmm. This dressing is perfect." Then after a pause, "Italy once. That's all, but I've been to Mexico and Canada."

"I've always wanted to go to Mexico. Where were you?"

"Baja California. It was a fishing vacation with my dad."

John drank a bit more. "After your mom died?"

"Yeah, about a year or so after. Just before I left for college." Claire paused and drank some wine. "How about you?"

"Oh, I don't fish."

She hit him in the arm. "No, silly," she laughed, "have you been to Europe?"

"France once, on a high school field trip. But I went to Egypt in graduate school."

Claire's eyes brightened. "I bet that was awesome."

"It was. Imagine living in one of the world's oldest human civilizations."

"How long were you there?"

John counted in his head while he chewed. "About a week in Giza and two weeks in Alexandria."

"Wow. I'm jealous." Claire grabbed another slice of cheese. She looked at John and thought to ask a question, but then stopped. She needed a strategy to open him up.

John looked down at his salad and ate a few bites in silence. He could feel Claire watching him.

A few seconds later, Claire freshened their wine glasses and raised her to toast. "Thank you for a wonderful dinner, John. A girl can get used to this."

John swallowed some merlot. "It's the only skill I have to offer."

"I have an idea," Claire suggested, "but first, let's finish this bottle." She emptied her glass in two large gulps. "Drink up."

John followed her cue and emptied his glass. Claire emptied the bottle in two equal portions and lifted her glass again "Bottoms up."

After kicking the first bottle John rose from the table and walked to the bar. "Do you want the same?" he gestured to Claire.

"Yes, if you like it, too."

"I do. It's nice with the cheese."

John corked the bottle and poured two new glasses. They let it breath in their glasses while nibbling on some Asiago. "So," he asked, "what is your idea?"

"Truth or dare!" she answered excitedly.

"Huh?" John responded quizzically.

"I want to play truth or dare. Three rounds each."

"Are you sure?"

"You're a closed book, John Diver. I want to get inside that head of yours. Three rounds. I'll even wait till you have another glass of wine to loosen you up."

As she smiled at him devilishly, he raised his glass and downed its contents fully. After swallowing, he resigned. "I guess I have no choice."

Claire poured a new glass for him. She drank a sip herself and sat up straight. "You can even go first."

John looked skeptically at her, and chewed a piece of bread for a moment. After sighing slightly he asked, "OK. Truth or dare?"

"Truth," she replied.

John paused for a moment, realizing that he had no idea what question he might ask her. He sipped his wine, and swirled the liquid in his glass. "What first brought you into my restaurant?"

Claire exhaled. "That's a good one. I remember walking by one day on my way to the post office. I liked your door, because my dad used to carve things as a hobby, and yours has that nice molding. A few weeks later, I saw a flyer for a reading group at the library. I didn't have a lot of friends in my department so I called the number just to see. I ended up talking to Jacob, and he told me that the club met at *De Terre*. I didn't put the two together until I showed up for the first meeting, but when I saw the door, I thought it was fate."

They toasted and drank together.

"Now my turn," Claire said, energized. "Truth or Dare?"

"Truth."

She then paused to think. "Let's stay on the same subject...what did you think when you first met me?"

Diver chewed the inside of his lip. "I thought you were far too young and too pretty to be hanging around the Hogues. I wondered if you were their sister." His response ended as quickly as it began.

Claire was unsatisfied. "Hmm. Well, I'll let you go with just that for now, John Diver. Your turn again."

"OK, truth or dare?"

"Truth," Claire answered.

"Are you planning to get your doctorate at another university?"

It was a question she had not foreseen. And, in fact, had not thought a great deal about since they had met. Claire found herself caught off guard. "I guess so," she shared, "I have some applications out. I had always thought I'd go closer to home so I could see my dad more. But..." She then stopped and dropped her eyes.

"But what?" John prodded.

"That was before I met you."

John raised his glass to his lips again. He could feel the conversation turning to a place he found uncomfortable. It was too personal. Too intimate. Too invasive.

When Claire spoke again, her voice was nervous. "I guess it's my turn again."

"OK," John followed.

"Truth or dare?"

"Let's stick with truth."

Claire looked directly at him, piercing his eyes. John was melting in her gaze. He felt himself giving up. Surrendering. Was it the wine? Was it her?

"Do you like being with me, John?"

John swallowed. His anxiety suddenly fell. "Yes, I do. All the time," he replied.

It was the easiest answer he had ever given.

"I do, too," she returned.

It was a first for them both. And each instinctively knew something had just changed. They kissed across the table and the air seemed lighter around them. The moment might have lasted five seconds, but would linger for the rest of the evening. They sat back, sighed and smiled, emptying their glasses once more. John's head was swirling a bit. Claire seemed sharp, even if her eyes had become glassy.

"One round to go," she smiled. "Your turn."

John smiled back. "No, you go again. Ladies first."

Claire finished the last piece of cheese on her plate. As she softly chewed she thought of her final question. "Truth or dare?'

"Truth."

"OK, John Diver. How did you get to this place?"

John was a bit confused. "What do you mean?"

"Answer however you'd like. You're one of the smartest men I've ever met. One of the most well-read, too. Yet, you left the academy. You left your studies. You chose to live the life of a hermit when you have so much to offer. I want to know why."

John emptied the second bottle of wine into their glasses and began his response.

"It was fate, I guess."

Claire smiled at him and shook her head. "You're drunk. I don't buy that for a minute."

"Maybe so," Diver exhaled. "But is was a decent answer, no?"

"Insufficient," Claire answered, shaking her head. "I want to go again."

"OK, but you're breaking the rules."

"Truth or dare."

John, now fairly drunk, smiled at her. "Dare."

Claire was done with her game. She was ready for something else. "I dare you to make love to me in your kitchen."

Twenty-one

So much to be done, Simon thought, but it need not be now. He looked up quizzically at the young man above him. His sight was blurred. His body was quite numb. He felt the realization that it was ending, but was surprised at the peace of it all.

The man above him — a boy really — could not have been twenty-five. Had they met before? There was something familiar in his face. Over his dark-blue uniform he shrugged off the medical pack hanging by a strap at his shoulder. A yellow hard case, into which he thrust his hands, produced two disks with thin cords. He was speaking. Simon could not make out the words. The young man's brown eyes were wide, and thin beads of sweat gently fell from the brows above them. If Simon could speak, he would tell him to worry not, to go to his lover, his wife, his children, and share ice cream sodas on a porch swing.

Go and enjoy your life, my son, this is what you can do for me.

He was unsure where he had fallen. It appeared to be his study, upon close inspection, but he had never seen the view from his floor. He presumed himself to be lying on the kilim his wife had purchased long ago, staring up at the ceiling light—or was it the sun?—now overwhelming his vision. He could not feel the stiff fibers scratching at his neck. He could not smell its wooly odor, its musty scent. He could not see his desk beside it. Only the distressed young man above him faded in and out of focus.

Come with me for a moment, young man.

The brackish waves slapped at the craggy beach a distance away from them. The Indian Ocean seemed endlessly frigid and aggressive. The sky a strange shade of brownish-blue. The markets of Zanzibar were as exotic as they were unnerving. It was a foreign place, about as foreign as possible to an American, Simon thought. It was a place of gathering, an island embedded with Hindus, Muslims, Coptics, Africans, Indians, Maasai, Bantu, Makonde, pirates, sailors, merchants, and pilgrims. As a white couple, he and Josephine were targets of the papasi, who assumed, or perhaps hoped, they were Americans. The papasi were savvy and extraverted, often using salacious humor in their pitches, but always accepted refusal begrudgingly. The Maasai were the best salesman, equally using their culture and gregariousness as a draw to unload beaded bracelets to tourists, or to sit for portraits in their regalia with western families. They talked on cellphones wearing kikoi, and spoke English well.

Naomba kukupiga picha? It was considered polite to ask before taking photos. The residents were conscious of their poverty in Tanzania, and sensitive about their exploitation by foreigners. The small children playing football in the streets with bare feet had none of this reticence, but the adults were altogether different. This part of Africa had skipped a generation of technology, going straight from having no electricity to the digital age. The evidence of this vast transition was overwhelming. Restaurants had no toilets, but offered Wi-Fi. There were no landlines, but cell reception was flawless. It was common for men to walk holding hands. Often in their other they were speaking on flip phones across continents in Swahili,

Afrikaans, Urdu, Greek, or Arabic. It was a scrappy and
industrious country, but their secrets were their own.

As they walked the narrow winding streets, not built
wide enough for a car, they passed stucco and brick
whitewashed structures never more than two stories high. They
were all clean but in various stages of disrepair, including their
ornately carved wooden doors. Scraps of metal often covered
holes in walls or roofs. There was constant sweeping throughout
Stone Town, the moving of dirt from one place to another. The
only escape from the dust was the water, as was evidenced by
the ubiquity of young children who swam off the dhows
anchored in the bay while their fathers crabbed.

It was Josephine's dream to come here, enticed by the
mythology of missionary David Livingstone, born in Blantyre,
the same town as her grandfather, who immigrated to America
after the First World War. On their tenth wedding anniversary,
Simon surprised her with tickets, and she surprised him with
news of her pregnancy. Several months later, what seemed the
far off daydreams of romance novels was their reality. They
toured spice farms and ate pilau. Amidst the slave markets and
crumbling mosques it was possible to imagine Hemingway's
tortured need for discovery, for an extant knowledge lying
somewhere just beyond reach, nestled in a crag between fear and
beauty.

Asambe omtanani, lilanga lisholile
Ambakathe ambakathe, ambakathe ambakathe

Simon was enthralled with the colorful khangas made
and sold by women in the markets, which was complemented by
shops bursting with elegant abstract carvings in dark ebony.
When a Persian rug store crossed their paths, they entered,
loosened by the romance of the city. It was there that she
purchased the kilim. For baby Levi, she said, wrapping it around
her waist. That night when they slept they heard the colobus
monkeys barking in the almond trees.

How fitting now that it should be the place where Simon
lay agape, immobile, prepared to join his family again. He

thought himself to be smiling and wondered if it confused the young man working furiously at his chest. He would understand someday, he thought, when he'd stuck it out long enough. Simon saw the faces of his young students, now surely grown, as they answered problems sheepishly in a corner classroom. He saw Tim, who was nearsighted. He saw Natalie, who was abused by her stepfather. He saw Jeremy, who went on to Dartmouth.

He saw Josie and Levi.

He saw John, stirring soup in *De Terre*.

And then he saw nothing more.

Twenty-two

He had gone too far. The right side of his mouth cascaded sweet carnage like a meat pillow, swollen beyond his molars. There was the slight satisfaction of pushing farther than he ever had, but it was dampened by reservation. He would take days to heal. As he pressed his tongue against the soft flesh he felt both comfort and shame — a tandem that had become familiar. He presumed his wounds to resemble a fighter's, although his flayed tissue remained hidden. Inside. Within. Privileged. A fighter fighting himself. He didn't remember the match. There was whiskey and loneliness and a chair beside the window. He did not recall the gnawing…the carving. The alcohol must have numbed him, leaving him unaware of the blood he swallowed with every sip. He hoped he could speak. Opening his mouth was agony. More than was normal. More than was pleasurable. More than he wanted.

John rubbed the steam from his medicine cabinet window. He rubbed his face waiting for the reflection to clear, and reached for his brush. After building a dam of foam in his soap dish, he moistened his three-day beard until a lather coated his skin. With a safety razor, he began to shave, left side first, then center, then right. Always the same. And always a cut or two when he rushed.

At first believing it was superior, he had shunned the new Machs and electrics long ago in favor of the old-school method. Double-edged razor blades. Badger-hair brush. Shaving soap. It might have been superior, he presumed, were he a more patient shaver. But after countless nicks, bleeders and burns, he found it still rather comforting in some way. Whether it was the potential danger, the pain, or its link to the past he did not know, but it was a ritual that had become his.

He decided to be methodical that morning. To pay attention. To be slow and considerate in his movement. Simon would have appreciated that. He was a man of great manners and grace. A throwback. And for John, he was a father figure in many ways, even if they had only met in adulthood.

He finished with only the smallest cut at his Adam's apple, a tough spot for sure. After bracing his cheeks and neck with a splash of witch hazel, he turned to his bedroom to begin dressing. Claire's sweater hung on a bedpost beside him. She was last there two nights prior, the evening before he received a phone call from a paramedic friend and customer of *De Terre*. He knew Simon from the restaurant, and was there at the end. He called John even before the coroner, which, in some way, made Diver feel significant.

After dressing in his only suit, a dark-gray polyester blend, he took a quick glance out the window to view the low clouds over the town, and headed downstairs to the side door. Walking over the sidewalk, he hung a sign on the glass door in the front of his restaurant. It read: "Closed to commemorate the life of Simon Pence." It was the first time John had ever closed *De Terre* unexpectedly, and he hated having a reason to do so.

He climbed into a Ford Taurus. Not owning a car himself, he had rented one the day before, thinking he'd want to make himself available to transport friends. John knew he was the closest thing to family Simon had left, and he took the responsibility to insure he would be honored in an earnest manner, similar to the way he lived. John had coordinated the wake with the assistance of the local funeral home. As for the funeral itself, Simon had left his wishes with his lawyer, along with a will. As in life, Simon was also fastidious in death.

As he drove, he looked about the town. It was unchanged, even in the gravity of this moment. Store windows were coated in frost. The snow bunched like sooted crystalline stones at the curbs. Smoke rose from the chimneys of houses as icicles grew on their gutters. It was two o'clock on a weekday, and the streets were fairly unpopulated. He noticed one young woman pulling her child in a sleigh across their front yard. Don't you know what has happened, John wondered. Don't you know that my friend has died?

Diver turned at a stoplight and drove down a newly paved street to a small group of apartment buildings. There he saw Lanny standing outside, waving to him as he pulled up. He wore a full-length black overcoat that looked quite handsome. As he got into the car, his eyeglasses fogged up from the change in temperature. It made John smile.

Lanny closed the passenger door. "Ugh," he sighed, "It's freezing out there. I hate the winter."

John replied, "You say that every year, Lanny. You're living in the wrong place."

Lanny wiped his glasses clean and exhaled. "That's true. But where else would I go?"

John continued slowly down the road. The plows had been out earlier, coating the roads with a dusting of sand. It crunched under the car's tires. What ice there was on the asphalt was coalesced to the center of the street on its yellow dotted line.

It was an afternoon that otherwise would have been comforting to John. He enjoyed the low hanging clouds that would drop out of the mountains, and the cutting wind that would bring tears to his eyes if he caught its direction just right. Smoke rose from fires in wood stoves. Crows sat at the tops of fence posts. It seemed as if the world had slowed down, bringing with it a reduction of its chaos, if only for the torpor of its creatures.

"How are you doing, John?" Lanny asked, breaking the silence between them.

"OK, I guess," John replied. "It's a strange day. Part shit and part solemn."

"Simon was a good man. I know this is a sad day, but in a way, I feel relieved. I always felt so bad for him that he had outlived his family — that he had to bury his wife and son."

John swallowed. "It was always there with him. You could read it on his face."

"I was there at his son's funeral. I don't know if I ever told you. I went to school with him. It was just after I got back into town. Simon remembered me. From all those years."

"I'm sure that comforted him," John replied. "Simon was old-school. He really cared about people. About touching people."

"I wonder how many of his students will be there today."

John had not thought of that. "Good question. It's hard to say. How many people who grew up here stick around these days?"

"Just on the farms mostly…but that's still a lot."

John had relationships with many of the farmers in town, but most of them were far older than he. It was rare to receive orders from anyone younger than fifty, which he had never considered deeply before. Was he witnessing the waning days of a local industry? A way of life? On one hand, he appreciated light banter with the older men at his loading dock. They cussed with no shame. They laughed mischievously at off-color jokes. They told stories of yesteryear. They smelled like the earth.

Were they the last heroes? The last of their kind? They were veterans of foreign wars, members of local lodges, occasional racists, and fierce defenders of their community.

John shook his head. No reason to grant them apotheosis, he thought. They simply lived by a different code, a code that was disappearing, like so many of the native languages of the area. All was being consumed by the empire, which, as Coetzee wrote, was only concerned with its future. The past was nothing but death. And the present, if immobile, was already the past.

As he came to the road's end, John hit his turn signal and entered the parking lot of the funeral home. There were a dozen cars in the lot, each covered with varying degrees of salt at the fenders. He recognized Claire's Honda and pulled beside it. As he turned the car off, a light flurry of snow blew across the windshield.

"Well," he said, unlocking his belt buckle, "here we are." They exited the car in silence.

A man with a kind expression opened the door for them, greeting them with sympathy. He wore a black suit and appeared openly genuine to the melancholy of the day.

"Welcome, Mr. Diver," he said. "We spoke on the phone. I'm Charles. Please let me know if there is anything I can do for you. I'm very sorry for your loss."

"Thank you," John answered, shaking his outstretched hand.

The foyer opened into a small chapel-like room. It was quite warm inside, and many bouquets of flowers, some real and some fake, appeared throughout the interior. Eight rows of folding metal chairs lined the space, separated by a central aisle. At each side of the room a large valence covered a window, allowing light to enter the room in a diffuse pattern. Diver then saw the casket on the stage, its lid opened widely, and, in front of it, Claire.

She saw him before he saw her, and was already walking to him.

When she met him, she pressed her hand into his and kissed him on the lips. "I'm so sorry, John", she expressed. Her eyes were red with tears.

She wore a dark-grey dress with black boots that ended just below the knee. Her hair was pulled back with barrettes. This moment between them was a first in many ways, he thought. They were publically affectionate. Of course, John knew that their romance was a poorly kept secret amongst their friends, and secret perhaps only in his illusions. Nonetheless, he wondered how many people in the room their embrace surprised.

But perhaps more importantly, this moment saw each of them as keepers of the other. Tragedy can define a relationship, either strengthening it or reducing it to nothing. It demands a reckoning, forcing one to examine the depth of one's affections. Unconsciously, one weighs selfishness against selflessness. Such are the rites of passage. John recognized, as they squeezed their hands together, that they had crossed a threshold. They still knew very little about each other. But John knew there would be time for them to learn more.

Claire dried her eyes on John's lapel and peered up at Lanny beside him. She hugged him and expressed her sympathy. Several seconds later, Liz appeared before John and hugged him deeply.

"I'm so sorry, John," she whispered, her voice audibly cracking.

"He really liked you, Liz," John replied. "You always lit his face up."

"He was the greatest gentleman I ever knew," she said, and then paused. "He's going to ruin men for me for the rest of my life. No one will compare to him."

Claire then took John's hand in hers as they walked to the front of the room and sat in a row before the casket. Lanny got up and kneeled before it silently. As John looked about the room, he saw fourteen people, several of whom he recognized. He nodded to several as their eyes met.

As the sky became more clouded the room dimmed slightly.

A few silent minutes later, as he bit into the sides of his mouth, John felt his chest tighten, and a wave of heat flush his skin. He recognized the panic from attacks he had long ago, but had forgotten for some time. He felt vulnerable in the open, and fought to control his fear beside Claire. He swallowed and stiffened his limbs as if to become stone. Claire's hand was on his thigh, which now trembled beneath it.

"Are you OK?" she asked.

John's face was pale. "Yeah," he replied, trying to be reassuring, "I'm all right."

As waves of blood seemed to flood his lungs, John breathed deeply, as he remembered a doctor's advice. You are in control, he reminded himself. You are in control.

Claire felt John's discomfort. She knew him better than he was aware. She knew his compulsions — his hair pulling, his biting. She knew he had nightmares. She wondered if he knew that he talked in his sleep. She had not told him yet — worried he would become self-conscious. She almost liked it. It was a reminder that he was next to her.

She pressed her hand into his thigh to relieve his shaking. She waited for him to cry.

John looked up to see Lanny return from the casket. The room was very quiet.

He looked at the elaborate stage before him, knowing that Simon's body was laid there before him. He had no desire to see it. He wanted to remember Simon in life. In fact, John suddenly become angry at Simon's passing. It was not the subject of psalms and songs, but a reminder of the brutality of life. Of its indifference…its random horror and infinite injustice. Alive and well were the torturers of men, sipping wine in mansions with their families. Alive and well were the terrorists, planning for eternal glory through the violence of faith. Alive and well were the mercenaries, trading blood for gold. Alive and well were the murderers justifying hatred behind their badges.

And gone was a man of dignity. And the son of a man with dignity. And the wife of a man with dignity. As if the world loathed them for their principle. Martyrs for laughable causes.

One such slap in the face could be treatable, if only over drunken rants that recognized the hypocrisy of human kind, but a war on two fronts was overwhelming. The greater enemy was the recognition that we are flies in spiders' webs, squirrels in the mouths of dogs, antelope in the jaws of lions. Heaven is a child's dream. The soul is an idea of philosophers locked in classrooms with red wine and wheels of cheese. There are no pleas answered in the remote caves of the earth, where we view shadows as reality and comfort each other for confessing sins to our gods so that they be erased from the record of our lives.

You are in control, John struggled to believe.

But such control was a myth. This reality was one that that humanity sought to grapple with yet simultaneously deny. In four thousand years we had come up with two answers—the invention of god and the creation of law, both of which required submission. It was the way we attempted to order the world…to give it meaning…to give it purpose. But even with such estimable goals we saw through the cracks. Like the wolves, we killed to survive. In times of hunger we ate our young. We changed gods and changed laws, and applied them differently in different situations. The greatest truths were subjective.

And now a great man was dead. A man who knew all these truths and still lived a life of radical decency. A man who was defiant by being gracious in the face of hostility. A man without whom *De Terre* could not exist.

John's pulse was as rapid and wild as his thoughts. His head hurt. His body hurt. His heart hurt. He had tried to make a difference. He had tried to feed the hungry.

He was done.

The goddamned world could starve.

He rose to use the restroom, excusing himself to Claire and wiping the sweat from his brow. His legs were shaky in the first few steps. As he reached the foyer again, a white-haired gentleman approached him. He wore a brown suit and tan tie with black checks. John did not recognize him.

"Excuse me, Mr. Diver?" he asked, extending his hand.

John swallowed, "Yes, have we met?"

"I've been to your restaurant once. My wife loved your risotto. But I'm here today for Simon. I was his attorney. My name is Roger Brownback."

"Hello, Roger. It's nice to meet you."

"I'm sorry it's under these circumstances."

"Yes, I understand. Did you know Simon long?"

"Thirty years," he replied. "He was a client and a friend."

"He will be missed," John replied, realizing the weakness of such a phrase.

"I was on my way out," Roger continued, "but I wanted to introduce myself. Simon told me a great deal about you. He loved you like his own son."

John struggled for a response. No words came.

Roger continued, "As you know, he has no surviving family outside of his daughter-in-law. He left you a sum of money in his will." With that, he took out a business card from his chest pocket and extended if to John. "Call my office next week, and I can review the document with you."

John took the card incredulously. "Thank you," he said with a sad smile. "Thank you for being here."

With that the man turned and left, and the frosty air from the outside rushed in as the door opened upon his exit. The cold reminded John that he was alive. The skin on his arms puckered, and he drew a deep breath. The spiders would go hungry today, he thought. If the world had no thought for him, he would have no more thought for it. He rose against its barbarity and walked slowly and dutifully back into the chapel. To his right, he saw his beautiful Claire. He smiled at her as he approached Simon's prone body on the stage.

As he looked down, a tear betrayed him.

Then another.

Twenty-three

The stack of hardcover books on her desk now numbered seven high. To their right was a disordered stack of graph paper, each with handwritten notes scrawled across their surface in blue and black ink. As she typed a few more words on her laptop, Claire caressed her forehead and winced her eyes from strain. She clicked save, and put the computer to sleep, sighing loudly.

"Are you finally done?" Liz called over, leafing through an Atlantic magazine.

"For today, anyway," Claire responded.

"I envy you. You have something to take your mind off of Simon."

"Yeah. It's not working particularly well."

"C'mon," Liz invited, "let's go make some dinner. I'm opening up another bottle of wine."

Liz walked across the living room into Claire's kitchen. Her cat sat hungrily on the counter, awaiting dinner as always. Liz scratched its head and grabbed the bottle of Rioja next to the stove and corked it. After replenishing her glass, she poured one for Claire.

"You know, if you told me a year ago that the great love of my life would be a seventy-year-old widower, I'd think you were crazy." She extended the glass to Claire and sat down on the sofa.

After swallowing a large gulp Claire responded. "You've yet to meet the great love of your life, Liz. He's waiting for you somewhere."

"You're lucky that you've found yours."

Claire took another long gulp of wine. "That's not something I know yet."

Liz was already tipsy. "But it's something you hope, right?"

Claire had no reason to hide. "Yes," she said, "I guess I do."

"And so I envy you again," she answered. "Now, what can we eat in this place?'

"I don't have much," Claire answered. "How about macaroni and cheese?"

"Homemade?"

"Sure," Claire smiled back, "by Stouffer's."

Liz emptied her glass. "Get it in the oven, girl."

They both walked into the kitchen. Claire opened the freezer and took out the frozen mass of noodles. Liz turned on the oven.

"Should I feed Cliff?" she asked, petting the tabby.

"Sure," Claire answered, "he's always hungry."

Liz filled the cat's bowl with half a cup of kibble and placed it on the ground. The cat jumped off the counter and meowed before trotting off to eat.

After placing their dinner in the oven, Claire leaned with her back against the sink. She could smell the oven warming.

"Want some baby carrots?" she asked Liz.

"Sure, I could use some vitamins."

As Claire grabbed a bowl from the cabinet Liz pondered aloud, "Do you think the reading group will continue?"

"I'm not sure," Claire answered. "I didn't think you liked Bill that much anyway."

"He's grown on me a bit. I found a really nice book on folk art yesterday in his store. He gave it to me for half-price."

"That was nice of him."

"And it wasn't sleazy either. He wasn't hitting on me or anything. I could see in his eyes that he was just sad like me."

"It's been a sad week," Claire said, crunching a carrot in her mouth. She offered the bowl to Liz. "Have some."

As Liz chomped on the vegetables she kept talking, "Are you seeing John tonight?"

"No, I told him I needed to work on my writing. The roads are really bad anyway. I'm not sure I'd want to be driving out there."

"I know. For all the snow we've got, the skiing is supposedly terrible right now. It's all hard-packed."

"Speaking of, Simon's death is hitting John hard. He's making it worse by bottling it up."

"That's pretty common."

"I know. It's frustrating though. I want to help him. He won't let me in."

"I thought he was getting better at that."

"Well, he is," Claire corrected. "I shouldn't say that he won't let me in. He just won't let me *all the way* in."

"Give him a little time," Liz comforted. "He doesn't wear his emotions on his sleeve. But he loves you."

"How do you know?"

"I saw it in his eyes at the wake," Liz answered. "There was no mistaking it."

Claire blushed.

"Has he not told you?" Liz asked.

"No."

"Have you not told him?"

"No. Well, almost."

"I don't know what you're waiting for," Liz stated.

Claire admitted she didn't know either.

"I'm sorry," Liz added after Claire's silence, "I didn't mean to get all into your business. She walked over to Claire and ran her hands through her hair. "You know I'm living my love life vicariously through yours, right?

Claire chuckled. "That's a first."

Liz laughed as well. "Maybe this is what I should do. Maybe I should let you make my romantic decisions for me. I keep making bad ones. You should just tell me what to do."

Claire spoke loudly. "Rule number one. Stop sleeping with lacrosse players."

Liz shook her head. "Never mind," she gestured, "you are relieved of duty."

Claire felt Cliff rubbing against her legs. She bent over and picked him up, groaning under his weight.

"Your cat is fat," Liz smirked.

"I know," Claire answered. "Let's go sit in the living room. We have a half-hour before dinner. Grab the glasses, will you?"

Liz grabbed both wine glasses and two bottles of wine. She placed them all down on the glass table in front of the sofa. "Let's not pretend we're not drinking all this, right? I'm just being efficient."

Upon pouring two fresh glasses Liz flopped down beside Claire. The cat purred between them.

"How is the thesis coming along anyway?" Liz asked.

"Pretty well. The PMA is being very helpful. With luck, it's possible they might even publish a catalog under their press using an essay of mine."

Liz grew excited. "Really?"

"They mentioned the possibility — at least the curator I've been working with did. I'm not sure how much clout she has."

"That's a big deal."

"Yes and no," Claire responded. "I do get a publishing credit, but there's no money involved. And it's not really in my field."

"Fuck it," Liz answered defiantly. "Let's toast."

They touched their glasses and drank deeply. The smell of cheddar cheese now faintly surrounded them.

Liz emptied the first bottle into their glasses. She'd be quite drunk soon if she did not eat.

"OK, big question now," Liz prefaced. "What are you going to do at the end of the term?"

"What do you mean?" Claire asked.

"You're graduating in May. You're going to hear from your Ph.D. programs any day now."

Liz looked at Claire pointedly.

"And?"

"And John, Claire," Liz pleaded. "What about John?"

Twenty-four

It was a bitter early March evening. Lanny emerged from the dining room lazily. "We might as well close, Chef. Bill and Jacob are all we have out there. The roads are sheets of ice."

John looked at the clock on his table. It read 8:50. The Rangers were beginning the third period against the Sabres.

"Why don't we join them for a drink, Lanny." he answered. "I'll shut down the grill."

After swallowing another bite of his Swiss cheese sandwich, John turned the burners of his flattop off and finished his third beer of the night. He pulled several quarter pans from his small steam tray and set them aside to cool. Atop his prep table there was a Louise Bourgeois monograph. He had bought it a Bill's bookstore shortly after she died. He had been fond of her work when he was a student, but like many things, he had forgotten her until he read of her death. On its cover she was photographed with a sculpture of a phallus. She was as irreverent as she was brilliant. Her absence left the world a more dreadful place. Another reminder that evil men live forever with new hearts stolen from young children. The good feed worms beneath the soil.

After turning off the salamander, John walked to the kitchen door and exited to the dining room.

Outside, Bill and Jacob sat next to the fireplace, with Lanny chatting beside them. John funneled to the bar and grabbed his bottle of Knob Creek, and slowly walked to the table with four glasses.

"Let's have a drink, shall we?" he said, placing the glasses on the table.

"Why thank you, John. How are you doing tonight?" Bill asked.

"About as good as you'd expect," John responded.

"I know what you mean," Bill replied. "As bad as it is out there tonight, I didn't want to stay home again."

"It's been a tough week," Lanny added. He pulled out a seat and took it. "How's your family, Jacob?"

"Good," he replied faintly. "My girl is graduating from middle school this year."

"That's nice," Lanny answered. "She'll be dating soon."

"Don't remind me, Lanny," Jacob said with a smile. "I want to send her to a nunnery."

John managed a partial smile while filling each glass with bourbon. They all recognized the Shakespearian reference, which might have precipitated a tangential exchange on any other night.

After pouring, John held his glass in the air. He remained standing.

"To Simon Pence."

The three raised their glasses in unison. "To Simon Pence."

After downing the ounce of bourbon they each rested their glasses on the table with dull thuds. John grabbed the bottle and filled his glass with two fingers.

"Anyone?" he asked raising the bottle aloft.

"I'll take one," Lanny said, "make it a double."

"I'm good," Jacob replied.

"As am I," Bill responded.

As John and Lanny continued to drink, Bill slouched over the table, moving closer to the other men. "He was an American hero, you know."

The table was quiet until John spoke. "Not a hero," he began, "heroes are flawed. He was a real human being. An authentic man who lived an ethical, moral, and dignified life. A man who refused himself hypocrisy or relativism. The kind of human we all think we are but fail to be. "

"But heroic in a sense." Jacob added.

"Yes," Diver agreed, "you are both correct, but only because such a person is so rare today."

"He was a rare soul," Bill said. "He lived his life in service to others, like his son."

"To have to bury your son," Jacob said, "it must have been terrible."

Lanny swallowed and put his glass down. He sighed. "My uncle killed himself on New Year's Eve. He left a wife and two kids. None of us ever understood why."

"I'm sorry to hear that, Lanny," Jacob offered.

Lanny shook his head. "Ahh, it's not about that. What I meant was to say that Simon would never have gone out like that. As tragic as his life was, he always looked to help other people. That was his reason for living."

"*De Terre* would not be possible without him," John added.

The table was silent again.

"Our mother is in hospice," Jacob spoke. "She has advanced Alzheimer's. I go to see her about once a month or so. She's mostly nonresponsive. Her skin is like paper. She has to wear a mitten on her right hand so she won't scratch her chest raw. There are sores all over her."

"She weighs about seventy pounds. Sometimes I don't remember what she looked like before," Bill added.

Jacob continued, "I don't let my daughter see her. I don't want that memory inside her growing up."

There was nothing anyone wanted to say.

"Is it right to hope someone dies?" Jacob asked. "Is it any more right to hope someone continues to live?

"Every man's life ends the same way." John whispered.

Bill cocked his head quizzically.

"Hemingway said that. The difference is in how we live."

"I live in too much fear." Jacob said.

"You're not alone," Lanny added. "I'm forty-four years old and I'm not even out."

John emptied his glass. He was growing dark. "We're all cowards. It's our nature."

Attempting a change of subject, Lanny turned to Bill. "Do you think your reading group will continue?"

Bill sighed deeply. "I hope so," he exhaled, "but I can't see how right now."

John bit his lip quietly as Jacob tapped his fingers in a musical pattern on the table. A loud snap from the fire pierced the room.

"You know, all the books we read," Jacob began, "they all have characters like Simon. The protagonists. The good guys. It's the story of our country. Someone should write Simon's story."

"The story of America is more myth than truth," John responded.

Bill interjected. "Yes, but let's reverse that."

"Does the world want truth?"

Bill perked up. "Well fuck 'em. We'll give it to them anyway. Here's an idea. I propose turning the reading group into a writing group. We will write Simon's biography. We will write the story of one of our country's greatest sons."

John was suddenly heartened. "The triumph of the best of man."

"The triumph of the best of man," Bill echoed. "Someone needs to tell the story."

John smiled.

Bill continued. "Who better to do it? We know where he worked. We can do interviews all over town. We can talk to his daughter-in-law. She's in Baltimore, right? We can request his birth records. His marriage records. I'm on Ancestry.com"

Jacob added, "I think this can really work. I'm sure Liz and Claire will be in."

"Bill was inspired. "And with self-publishing software now, we can develop everything ourselves. All we need is a laptop."

"And the facts."

"Well, I can help. I know a bit about his father," John offered.

"Perfect. Let's toast again." He raised his almost empty glass high. "To Simon Pence."

"To Simon Pence." They responded.

"That's a good way to end the night. I'll write up a strategy with some bullet points," Jacob said. "Bill, we better get home. I just saw a plow go by so the timing's perfect."

"Can you guys take me?" Lanny asked. "I'm just a mile down."

"Sure."

"Thanks. Give me just a minute and I'll grab my coat."

Lanny and Jacob both got up. Jacob stretched out his arms in a yawn as Lanny pushed in his chair. He had drunk several shots of bourbon very quickly. Having not eaten that night, he felt himself mildly drunk.

John rose, "I'll come with you, Lanny."

As the two entered the kitchen, Lanny walked to his locker by the restroom. "John," he said, opening the thin metal door, "you probably know by now that I didn't get my loan."

John turned to him. "I saw the SOLD sign on the property."

"Well I'm about done, John," Lanny sighed. "This town has no place for my dreams."

"We can try at another bank, Lanny."

Lanny walked to John with his head down. "No. It's over. That was my last shot."

John stood firm. "Don't give up. You never give up. That's what makes you, you."

"There comes a time, John, when the time to dream is over. Dreams have windows. Mine has closed." He put his hand on John's shoulder. "Thanks for the bourbon."

As he walked out of the kitchen John heard Buffalo score in overtime.

"Shit."

Twenty-five

You do not go to the barber. You do not wish to hear their questions. They looked shocked, and wonder aloud if you are aware of your appearance. You want to tell them that you are sick, that you have had surgery, or that you burn you hair in Yahi ceremonies to honor the dead. They ask you what you would like. They know what you already know — that the only answer is to remove it all, and that is your job, not theirs. You want to keep your hair long, to cover the baldness behind your ears and the scars at the nape of your neck. Make me look passable, you say. Make me look human. For this miracle I will pay you handsomely, and excuse myself from your presence for another year. They are the keepers of your secrets, but they are sickened by you. And like strangers in elevators, you share nothing, and wait to be out of the door.

For months now, John wanted to remove the mirror Lanny had mounted on the wall. It sat almost perfectly opposite him as he paced his line between the range and the grill. He looked older in it than he should, which he blamed on the yellow fluorescent lights above him. But in truth, it was more accurate than he cared to believe. He peered at his portrait. The figurative painter Gustave Moreau had said that paint was the language of god. Probably because neither was real. Were he to draw himself, would he render his face more pitiable or more handsome? Would his marks be gestural or pointillist? Would the choice even matter?

John turned and looked up at the clock. It was getting late in the day. Lanny would be in soon to stock the bar and service the tables in the dining room. On Wednesday nights, the town's firemen ate for half-price, and while they were a small group, several always stopped by with their wives or girlfriends. They were mostly younger men, whose fathers fought fires as well, and who stayed for their love of the community. In the winter, most of their calls were over creosote sparking in chimneys. In the past, farmers used to burn their fields, but the regulatory costs had all but killed that practice long ago. Now, the company held open houses when the weather was nice, and hosted prevention days for the local schools. On Independence Day each year, the 500-horsepower hook and ladder engine would lead the parade down Main Street, and the kids received plastic red helmets.

As the clock turned to 4 p.m., John yolked a dozen eggs through the fingers of his right hand into a wide steel bowl. He reserved the whites and placed them in his reach-in. He turned to his range, poured four ounces of chardonnay into a sauté pan, and placed it over full heat. As the wine began to simmer, he added one finely diced shallot, freshly cracked pepper, a pinch of garlic, and half a cup of fresh marjoram. After reducing the mixture by half, he spooned in one healthy tablespoon of tomato puree and mixed with a whip to incorporate. He then turned off the burner to let the reduction cool.

Grabbing the steel bowl, he placed it over a steam bath and whipped the yolks firmly. After five minutes of constant whipping over the heat, the yolks thickened and lightened in color. With his left hand, John reached for a two-ounce ladle and poured clarified butter into the yolks in a smooth and slow stream. As the yolks emulsified with the oil, he added the butter more quickly, until a thickened glossy finish marked the sauce.

He then scraped the wine reduction into the bowl with a spatula and incorporated it, adding salt to finish.

The Sauce Choron would top his special that night—a thick slice of grilled pumpernickel topped with two slices of beefsteak tomato and a six-ounce tempeh burger, atop which he would place a duck egg sautéed over easy. The sandwich would be served open faced and covered with the sauce and diced scallions. Fried beets chips and cornichons would round out the plate. It was a variation of a popular special he offered monthly. A gut buster of sorts, that was a favorite of those with hearty appetites, or the affluent deadheads with the munchies who would sometimes appear out of the mountains on weekends.

John reserved the sauce in a covered quart-sized insert, leaving it beside the range near, but not too close, to the ambient heat of the oven. As he turned back to his prep table he glanced at the business card of Roger Brownback, whom he had called earlier to make an appointment. He seemed a very amenable man, the kind of man Simon would trust and befriend. It had taken John some time to call, for reasons he could not easily recognize, but upon doing so he was reassured by the lawyer's warm speaking voice. Whatever Simon had left him, John would learn of tomorrow morning.

It was possible John had not called earlier because it reminded him that Simon was in fact dead. If he could just keep dicing chayote, kneading bread or thinking of Claire, then he could forget that his friend was gone. He could keep pretending that one day Simon would enter the dining room for his soup du jour and cocktails like always. John understood this delusion, however, and ultimately refused its indulgence. There was another image he had trouble shaking—one that had stayed with him for several weeks since the funeral.

During the first hour of Simon's wake, six older men entered together. They were dressed in workman's clothes that were clean but well-worn. No one of them was younger than seventy, and three looked closer to ninety. John did not know any of them, nor had he ever seen them before. As they entered, each walked to the body and gave their respects individually, but quickly. After their prayers, they walked to the west parlor of the manor and sat with their hats in their laps, saying very little.

John welcomed a few guests and talked with acquaintances, turning his attention away from the men. The room had become slightly crowded, with a stream of Simon's former colleagues from the public school entering and introducing themselves. Claire stayed beside him supportively, and Lanny also remained near. Bill and Jacob entered soon thereafter, as did some younger families, whom John presumed to be Simon's former students. While words were difficult, and phrases repeated, the room took on a warm ambiance.

It was then that John needed some space and excused himself to walk around the rooms of the house. He struggled with anger and with sadness, and wandered without knowing into the room inhabited by the older men who had come earlier.

He sat down in an armchair opposite them in the large room. They were drinking coffee quietly. The room was warm, and the sound of a steam radiator was audible in the silence. As John observed them he could see in their faces the tired but proud expressions of each. They did not speak. Their countenance was telling...it seemed that each had been to ten funerals that month alone. This was a habitual component of their lives. It was their meeting place. The world was slowly taking things from them piece by piece—their jobs, their health, their bowels, their homes, and now their friends and family. He imagined that they wondered which of them was next. But they did not seem worried, nor did they seem emotional. It was as if they recognized the end of their lives and welcomed the end of pain, the beginning of peace.

Their hands were calloused, and while their fingers were clean, John could see the residue of the earth beneath their nails. Their skin was dark and cracked, and their white hair perfectly combed. As if a kind of honor guard for the townspeople, they sat at attention for the souls they would soon meet. One of the men met his eyes, and nodded his head in sympathetic poise. That glance, that single glance, was more profound than all the words Diver would hear that day.

Twenty-six

Having climaxed, John felt himself growing soft inside
her. Claire lay beside him, unwilling to let him go. They were
familiar now with each other's rhythms, communicating with
their bodies in ways that required no words. John enjoyed
watching her belly, with its gentle bump, arching and tensing on
top of him as it moved back and forth in waves. Her breasts, like
buoyant pearls, bobbed over his shoulders. He exhaled deeply,
now numb, and closed his eyes, as the smell of her hair
enveloped him.

When he woke again she was reading next to him. She
held a thin hardcover book titled *18th-Century Pennsylvania Law*
by Thomas Grotte. She looked up and smiled as she noticed him
stirring.

"Good morning, sleepyhead."

John rubbed his eyes. "What time is it?"

"Ten thirty," she replied. "I must have worn you out."

He looked at her. "You always do. What are you
reading?"

"Thesis research."

"Looks exciting."

She furled her eyebrows at him. "Says the man who just fell asleep on me."

John propped his pillows and sat up in the bed. The sun was now illuminating her shades in a way that marked the waning of winter darkness. The crocus flowers were beginning to pop up from the seemingly dead earth. Clearer skies still made for bitterly cold nights, but the snow at last was ending. When he turned his head, he noticed a cup of coffee on the bedside stand. It was black and strong, contained in a white mug stamped with linear designs. He reached for it happily.

"Thank you for making coffee," he said, sipping the dark liquid.

"You're welcome, sweetie." she answered.

"Tell me about your book."

She put the hardcover down on her lap and grabbed her coffee. She liked it with milk. After drinking a bit she smiled at John and turned on her side.

"So my guy, John MacPherson, remember? After he goes to Philadelphia, he builds a mansion. He wants to get in with the city elite. He hosts parties with his wife, Margaret. But he's essentially a pirate, so is gone for long periods of time at sea. His wife is left with the children. She gets lonely. He's never around. So she ends up having an affair."

"Really?"

"Yeah. Scandalous for that time. And it's with an influential man. He's a doctor."

"This is getting good."

"Yep. So, somehow MacPherson finds out about this. And he takes away her keys to the house. He locks her out."

Claire sipped at her coffee, pausing for a moment before continuing the story. "But hell hath no fury like a woman scorned. She gets her lover, the doctor, to have him declared insane. They get a police squad to the house to have him committed to a sanitarium. After a scuffle, the police arrest him and take him away."

"And he's just got the one arm, right?"

"Yeah."

"That's fascinating. A one-armed insane pirate. This must have made for some good town gossip."

Claire's eyes were bright and clear. "Well, here's the thing. After Margaret gets the keys to the house back, she gets him released."

"Huh?"

"Yeah. They make up."

"So it was all about the house?"

"This is my contention. It's not about the house. It's about the keys. When MacPherson took away her keys he took away her identity. They were a metaphor for her sense of belonging and affiliation. They were emblematic of her family and her safety."

"And what happened after he got out?"

She sighed. "Well, eventually they got divorced. That's why I'm looking at the law. I want to know what rights she had, if any."

"I imagine most women did not own property."

"He remarries later. But Margaret just kind of disappears in the records after that. I've lost her trail."

As he let Claire's words sink in, he remembered his own experience in graduate school. The nights of fruitless searches. The want for citations. The dead ends.

"You could be like Thucydides, Claire."

"The Greek guy you like? What do you mean?"

"In his *History of the Peloponnesian War,* he admits to not being present for all the speeches and actions of the war. So he kind of acknowledges to making some things up."

Claire looked at him sarcastically. "I guess he wasn't subject to peer review."

"True. Though, you know, whenever archaeologists had disputes about ancient cultures where the art conflicted with writing, they chose writing as the authority."

Claire paused and put her arm on John's chest. She looked into his eyes, glazing at one, then the other, in an attempt to bring him out of the shell he lived in.

"John," she pleaded, "be serious with me. You know more about most things than people in my classes. Why did you leave school when you were so close to your Ph.D.? Don't you ever wonder about where you'd be now?"

John knew he should respond by giving a piece of himself to her. She deserved to know him, but he greatly feared that there was so little to know behind his pretense. Relationships were built and destroyed based on things that were shared. But what if the truth just exposed his emptiness? He swallowed down his fear of being vulnerable. "I can't really point to anything specifically," he offered. "Haven't you ever just lost momentum?"

"Sure," Claire agreed. "Every day."

"I don't mean in an everyday fashion," John said. "I mean has your whole life ever just lost momentum?"

"I don't know what you mean."

"I guess I don't either exactly. But it's the best way I can explain it. It doesn't happen right away, so it's hard to notice it in real time. It starts day to day, then week to week, then month to month, and suddenly you wonder what has happened. Over time the things that meant a lot to me just stop meaning much of anything. It wasn't that I stopped caring…I just wondered why I should care to begin with."

"Did you have anyone to talk to? Anyone close to you?"

"Not close enough. But back then it wouldn't have mattered to me. I was losing touch with the world."

"But why?

John shrugged, "Why not?"

"I'm not immune to hopelessness, John. That's how I felt when I lost my mother. But we go on, don't we? We find happiness in small things. Despite the rest of the world."

"This is what I was worried about. That when you opened me up, you'd find nothing inside."

"That's not how I feel."

John ran his hand through her red hair. "All I can say now is that I'm happy to be right where I am."

"So you care about things again?"

"Yes."

"About me?"

"Yes."

"About school?"

John grinned. "About your school."

Claire smiled. Though not perfect, the answers were the ones she had hoped for. Honest. She kissed him and rubbed her face against his scratchy chin, smiling. "I need to tell you two things, John Diver."

"What things?"

"The first is that I've been accepted into a doctorate program. I leave this summer."

There was silence between them for a moment. John felt a pit in his stomach. "What's the second?"

Claire was very direct. "The second is that I love you."

Twenty-seven

As John sat in the waiting room of Roger Brownback's office, he studied the gray wall bearing a print of Monet's *Water Lilies* opposite him. It was well-framed, double-matted and tucked behind nonglare glass. Not a bad choice for office art, and far better than a shitty abstract textile to match the furniture. Two leather chairs framed the floor below it. He fumbled his fingers over each other as his hands rested in his lap. Monet was the least subversive of the Impressionists. He was one of the few whose career was immensely successful during his lifetime, allowing him comfortable means in the later phase of his life. While Diver admired the deftness of his hand, he preferred the work of Manet and Toulouse-Lautrec for their edgier subject matter. For respite, he would take Caillebotte, esteeming urban scenes over rural ones. Monet was safe. Too safe.

Diver wondered if the reason he studied the arts wasn't his fondness of sourcing the accomplishments of other people. Was his penchant for quoting just a way of not speaking for himself? Did he take cover behind the words of others? It was safer, he had to admit, for often, John quoted not to illuminate an inquiry, but to deflect it. In a strange way he was reminded of

Rousseau's *Letter to D'Alembert,* in which he objected to the theater as substitute for civic responsibility. Diver lived his life in books, and took action in his mind. Humanity was neither worth saving or condemning. He was not its savior, nor was he its judge. He was simply a cook.

Tolstoy once wrote that above all things, thinking makes men suffer the most. He was an inspiration of imagist writing, who even in the bleakness of the Crimean War could describe a soldier's jacket with three full paragraphs. Would such a genius trade his suffering for sciolism? Was it not the fate of all great men and women to bear some pain and isolation? Was this an elitist conceit? Is this why the Pharaoh lived apart from his countrymen? Is this why he was judged against the feather of Maat and feared being eaten by the god Ammit? Upon his death, as he sang to the hall of justice "I have not been deaf to words of truth!" did he not see the Field of Reeds in the distance? In their conversations, Simon would often remind Diver that there is no verb for "to not think" in the English language. If this was true, why, amongst the general populace, was it so apparent that thinking was no longer considered work, and that work required so little thinking?

At that moment, Mr. Brownback opened the door to his office, walked into the foyer, and extended his hand to John.

"Hello, John. Sorry to keep you waiting."

"Hello, Roger. No trouble at all. I was enjoying your print."

Roger looked up at the Monet. "My wife bought me that for my birthday. We went to France in the summer, and saw that painting in the Louvre."

"That's nice…really thoughtful," John replied.

As Roger ushered him into his office, John noted the many photos of his family on the desk and shelves around him. It appeared he had three daughters, who, like his wife, all had blonde hair.

"Please have a seat," Roger offered. "This shouldn't take long."

As John sat, Roger leafed through some paperwork on his desk before stopping at one page in particular. "So, John, just a few formal things to start. Simon left his will and affidavit with me. As you know, when Simon died he had only one relative, his daughter-in-law, Amy, to whom he left most of his assets. However, he also named you in his will. I have discussed the will with Amy and she is not contesting any of Simon's wishes, so we are in a good place and the probate process has been moving along for a few weeks now." He then thumbed to a new page and looked up. "I'd like to read Simon's final words to you."

John sat attentively, wondering what could possibly be said.

"John Diver," Roger began, "After my boy was lost to me, you became my second son. At a time when I had so little, I found so much in *De Terre,* and even more in your friendship. If my math is correct, I believe that you should owe somewhere in the vicinity of sixty thousand dollars on your mortgage. Knowing this, I leave to you whatever sum necessary to pay if off. As I was your partner in life, so I will remain your partner in death. Know that I loved you, and that I wish you more happiness than you can bear."

John stared blankly at Roger, as if what he read could not be true. He looked at the wall to his right. It was filled with shelves of hardbound books. He swallowed and attempted to speak. "I don't know what to say," he uttered.

"Simon thought of you very affectionately, John. He instructed me to verify your loan payoff amount. I'll need the bank information so I can make out the check directly."

John blinked, speechless.

"John?"

"Yes. Sure," he answered. "My account is at the credit union. I can fax the info over to you later today."

"Thank you, that would be great. I have other some paperwork for you, including a legal form called a "consent to probate." Now, according to the law, you have the right to contest the will if you desire."

John smiled incredulously and shook his head. "I have no desire to do that."

"OK, please sign this form for me then…with your signature here, and here." He handed John a pen.

"Once I have your other paperwork, which is mostly for tax purposes, I can petition the court to be appointed executor right away. As far as wills go, this one is fairly simple. With luck, *De Terre* will be yours in about three weeks," said Roger.

John shook his head in disbelief. "That's incredible."

Roger stood up. "Perhaps we can celebrate with dinner."

"Yes."

"So please fax me the completed forms when you have the chance. The sooner I get them, the sooner we can proceed."

"I'd like to contact Amy," John added. "My friends, Simon's friends, will be writing a book about him. We'd like her to be involved."

"That's admirable. Her information is privileged, but if you'd like I can forward her your number so that she can contact you directly."

"Yes, please. I'd appreciate that."

He shook Roger's hand and, exiting the room, Diver found himself reflecting back on the *Water Lilies*. For Monet, they were symbols of natural beauty. For Roger, they were a symbol of his wife's love. For Simon, *De Terre* was a symbol of family. For John, it had been a place to hide.

Twenty-eight

The first scent of spring touched Lanny's nose. To most, it would be imperceptible, simply a stiff breeze touched by the slightest humidity. But Lanny caught the fragrance of the chestnut trees with their catkins beginning to bud. They were favorites of his, and although he did not prefer their meat, their pinkish white flowers were lovely emblems of his home. The crocuses had come and gone. Lilies of the valley could be seen now along the driveways of many of the simple A-frame homes. Tulips would be next. Asparagus would soon be found in the local markets, along with greens and garlic.

In the town park, down jackets had given way to their lighter counterparts. He was there to feed the last of the Canadian geese, who would soon be gone north. But that morning, even with a large swan in view, he paid closer attention to the several families enjoying the late morning sun. A gaggle of children were busy navigating the jungle gym in knitted caps and hoodies, while their mothers watched and texted from the benches. On quick glance, it was a scene not unlike many throughout modern America, but one could see the playground features in slight disrepair, surrounded by some sizeable boulders, left there ages ago by glaciers, that would be considered dangerous in wealthier suburban enclaves. The kids here were tougher, Lanny thought. They had to be. The world was growing more inhospitable.

Two young boys, presumably brothers, had caught his eye. They couldn't have been more than ten years old, and they were scaling the geodesic dome with vigor. In a perfect world, they, and their parents, would be the perfect clients for The Family Kitchen. He could imagine them knee deep in chocolate and flour, stirring brownie batter with a kind of zest that Facebook was made to document. Their mother was fastidiously calling to them to be careful, to stop hitting each other, to come down from so high.

But they were having too much fun. Everyone in the park knew this. And even their mother, in quiet acceptance, was happy to see them get some energy out of their systems. The older of the two was protective of his younger sibling, even as he goaded him into climbing faster. They were close. They hadn't lived long enough to begin hating each other. They screamed and shouted boyish things. Cowboys and Indians. Allies and Axis. The other children in the park fell in line behind their charisma. Indeed, Lanny was also transfixed by them — until a particularly daring Mallard squawked at his lack of attention.

Lanny knew he would never have children of his own. He would never be married and raise a family. This did not overly sadden him. It was simply not a reality for him. And that was OK. Everyone had their place and everyone had their purpose. But what he never expected was to be shut out of his dream. To be denied a role in which he was at least family adjacent. Not twice.

In his past, amidst the gritty eastern boundary of San Diego County, pushed up against the edge of El Cajon, he worked at a local YMCA in an afterschool program where he read books aloud for the blind and hearing impaired, and, for that matter, anyone else who cared to join. At least half of his audience was children newly transplanted from Tijuana or Rosarito, not more than twelve years old, who were learning

English word by word from Kenneth Grahame and Edward Stratemeyer. It was something he fell into, having been recommended by the bartender of a popular breakfast joint where Lanny also waited tables on weekends. In it he found fulfillment, and was relieved to be away from the drug-addled crew at The Pancake Cabana. He read awkwardly at first, surrounded by frantic pairs of feet and arms in the carpeted basement of the basketball gym. But soon he grew to look forward his afternoons with the kids.

Some of them he got to know well. There was seven-year-old Julia, whose eyeglasses rivaled the thickness of bulletproof glass. Her mother, Jane, dropped her every Thursday before going to work. She was a nurse at St. Joseph's Medical Center. There were twins, Roberto and Florentino, whose exasperated mother, Ella, would drop them while she worked at an ESL class in an upstairs classroom. Lanny was a de-facto babysitter for them, often struggling just to keep them sitting for an hour at a time. He was building memories, he felt, trying to spackle over a crack in the crumbling infrastructure of the American family.

His job ended soon after the day one of the fathers, Hector, picked up his daughter from the group. Sarah's father, to be specific. Lanny had been reading to Sarah for several months. At eleven years of age, she was classified as learning disabled, having severe dyslexia. She spent most of her school day in a resource room, but she was in danger of being moved to a special school across the city. When Hector came to pick up his daughter he was cordial enough, and showed no outward signs of hostility. But soon thereafter, Lanny was called to meet his program director. A complaint had been filed against him, questioning why an adult man would be spending time with vulnerable children in such an unsupervised manner. The complainant asked for Lanny's qualifications, which were a matter of public record in the nonprofit world. When his supervisor could find no higher education in Lanny's CV, he was intimidated by the administration into giving his resignation.

And so it was, in the great state of California, that a man lost his job to an unfounded accusation. Lanny was not the first nor would he be the last. He knew this, which was why he was hurt but not angry at the predicament. He knew he couldn't afford to stay there much longer anyway. In America, you have to pay for beauty, and San Diego had it in spades. But before heading back to his birthplace, and with it, his hopeful rebirth, he couldn't help but conduct his journey in a most meandering way.

If Sarah's father had suspected Lanny of sexual deviance, he could not have been more misdirected. Even when Lanny found himself in Chicago several months later, he was still uninterested in relationships. There, again through a restaurant co-worker's invitation, he was working as a stagehand in a production of *The Normal Heart* by Larry Kramer. Most of the cast was openly gay, and even under their umbrella Lanny was often reserved and quiet, speaking with them professionally, as if in an unremitting job interview. He was happy there, however, and after some coaxing entered into his first loving relationship with an older man. At heart though he was a country boy, preferring *Brokeback Mountain* to *The Rushes*. He was never political. Never an activist. Never tied to the plights of a cause. He was as surprised as most to learn about AIDS. He was as unfamiliar as most with the Stonewall Inn. He shunned the parades. He snubbed the clubs. Ultimately, the noise and sweat of the city closed around him. After growing apart from his partner, he began his long, three-year drive home.

During that time, he remembered with fondness his days of the Y. He thought about a future. One with fixed goals and a permanent address. Soon after reaching the quiet foothills of his old home, he met John Diver and began working at *De Terre*.

He watched the more aggressive of the two boys reach the summit of the jungle gym, while a new band of toddlers arrived in the sand pit. The day was becoming unusually warm for that time of year, and jackets were shed across the playground. Several of them would have been perfect guests of The Family Kitchen, as would have been Julia and Florentino, Sarah and

Roberto. He thought for a moment of what could have been, before throwing the last of his bread to the birds.

Lanny loved working at *De Terre*, and knew that he had a special friendship with John. He recognized that he kept John balanced, and that he was a source of optimism in John's life. He could have easily worked there forever, had he not dared to dream. That was the problem with dreams, he mused, they trumped reality. And now that his dream was crushed, he could not go back to the way things were. Besides, he thought John would be OK. He had Claire after all—someone who could take good care of him and moderate his depression. If only John would let her. But, as painful as it was, Lanny could not stay for him. Things had changed. His die was cast. It had come up craps.

Twenty-nine

Diver reached for the half-empty bottle of bourbon in front of him, causing his head to throb from the sudden movement. One more finger, he thought, and then I'll pass out and feel better in the morning. Sunlight was always better than the dark. Darkness had been his enemy for some time. Years, maybe decades. It was when his anxieties attacked. When insomnia mocked him. When fear would not let him find peace.

He flashed back twenty-four years ago. He saw two medics in the hallway. It was an otherwise fine day, until that moment, when he heard the school announcer ask for John Diver to please report to the nurse's office. He was in senior English class. His favorite at the time. Seated next to no one in particular. His old friends, the ones he chose poorly, were no longer a part of his life. Neither were the smart kids, nor the jocks, nor the nerds, nor the goths. He rose with his books and left the room with a pass from his teacher, completely unprepared for the next week of his life.

As he opened the nurse's office door, he saw his mother — the first time in several weeks — the medics, and the school's psychologist and principal sitting in a semicircle of chairs. Their faces were adorned with looks of concern, or at least what they believed looks of concern should look like.

"John," the psychologist began, "we've found something that causes us great concern. We are here, your mother included, to help." While he spoke, John could see that he held a notebook of his, which was formerly in his locker. It was the notebook in which he wrote his poetry. Bad poetry to be sure. But poetry rife with vulnerability. Songs of suicide and isolation. Sadness. Purposelessness. Loss.

"We are concerned that you want to hurt yourself," he continued.

It was the start of a bad afternoon.

The remaining conversation was unclear. John did not offer much…and wasn't allowed to try, frankly. Minds were made up. Liabilities were protected. Lines of his poems were read aloud as if being entered into court records. John winced at the poor phrasing. The lack of timbre, of inflection. His words sounded even worse without being read with the certain disaffection with which they were written. There were accusations of drug use. Of anti-social behavior. Where did he sleep when he didn't come home? Had he come to school drunk last week? Why had he stopped playing sports? John was incredulous. He had his own questions. How was his notebook found? When were his rights violated? Why was he being made to face this tribunal?

The administrative collective had contacted the psychiatric ward of the local hospital. They had mutually decided that John was to join them for a week as an in-patient. This was the start of what would become an era of mass shootings, of events that, after occurring, were always defined by an oblivious community wondering what could have been done. Never mind that such events were the confluence of increasing social stresses, powerlessness, hormones, and easy access to guns. No, instead experts were in agreement that individuals were to be rooted out, that profiling would benefit the collective. Forget the internal review, the problem was deviation from the norm. John was a warning shot to the student body. The adults would not be caught unaware. He was committed with his parent's signature. In what seemed a moment's notice, he was reclined onto a gurney and wheeled into an ambulance in front of the school. As John looked up at the windows of the school he could see a majority of its two hundred and forty students staring at him, mouths agape, through the windows. It was quite a scene. The rumors started instantly.

And so it was that John Diver became interred. His file? Suicidal. Depressed. Anti-social. THC positive. LSD positive. He managed to interpret words off the chart of his doctor, a thin man with an overgrown moustache and wire-framed glasses. In the next several days, Diver decoded countless Rorschach tests. A bird. A tank. A fishing boat. He answered countless questions. No, he didn't think of the future. Yes, he did feel pressure to fit in. He also read. He watched movies. He took medication. He ate Jell-O. When it rained, he watched birds snatching the caterpillars off the sills.

As an unintended result of his therapy, John learned to distrust himself, his decisions, and his judgment. He learned to distrust people...people who exposed him, who gave him up, and who pointed and laughed at him like a sideshow clown as he was led away to the hospital. He learned to withdraw, to withhold. *You need to learn how to pick your friends*. He never knew this would be his omen.

That hospital was also the place he first learned to bite himself. It started innocently, just some pressure on his lower lip to delay a response here or there. But soon it became more severe. He found that he enjoyed inflicting pain upon himself, gnawing the inside of his mouth until it bled. When his skin needed to heal, he began to pull out his hair. It kept his hands busy to abrade his curls and pull at the coarse split ends. When the hair on his head was too short or too damaged to pull, he turned to his nose and forearms, which were more difficult to pluck, but more exquisitely painful. Soon his ticks engrossed him, and he was their servant.

His sterile gray room oppressed him. He was sure the color was selected scientifically. It mandated neutrality. If he had entered the ward healthy, the hospital only served to make him sick. So it often was, that good intentions (had the intentions been good?) backfire. He was stripped naked, left weakened and angry. When he was finally released, he was shaken. He immersed himself in books. Kerouac. Bukowski. Aleister Crowley. He sought refuge in the formerly subjugated, hoping to find kindred spirits. He left his home for good. He sometimes slept in the school's locker room, giving its night custodian money to keep him quiet. At graduation, he received a creative writing award. Had the irony eluded them? After throwing his cap, he drove south and never looked back.

Decades later, in the fuzz of the liquor, Diver scanned his apartment. In it he had few possessions. Apart from a dresser full of clothes, a heavy jacket, and some small appliances, his books totaled the most of its space. Claire's sweatshirt, like the relic of a goddess, was draped over a small TV in the common room. She frequently found it cold in his structure, which was surrounded by thick brick walls that shut out the sun.

He had come to a decision. It had actually arrived before that moment, but was nonetheless made easier to accept by the drink. He smiled knowing that he had conquered their programming. In spite of their efforts, he would succeed by his own definitions. There would be no summer menu for *De Terre* that year. There would be no plum tomato tarts, no arugula salads. There would be no more Simon, and no more firemen and no more reading group. Most of all, there would be no more hiding. He had found a rope to pull him away from his anxieties, and at the other end was a lovely girl. If he could not trust himself, he would trust her.

He would share the stories of his life with her. He would give himself up to something greater than himself. He would live.

Thirty

Claire, still a bit sleepy, curled her hair between her thumb and forefinger as she placed her phone to her ear. It was an early Sunday morning, but the sun was quickly warming the sofa through the bay window in her living room. She wore shorts and one of John's V-neck tees, which he frequently donned under his chef's coat in the kitchen. The room was quiet, as was the building. Most of her neighbors were either still sleeping or at church. John had left late the night before, needing to record inventory for most of the day. The reading group would be meeting later, working on collecting the stories of Simon's life.

"Hi, Daddy," she chirped as the she heard the ringer pick up.

"Klara. How good to hear from you. How is my daughter today?"

"Good, Daddy. How was mass?"

"It was nice this week. Everyone is excited about the new pope."

"Thanks great, Daddy." Claire paused, almost too excited to tell him. "So, I have some good news."

"What is it?'

"I got in."

She heard her father exclaim with joy. "I'm so proud! I never had any doubt."

"I got the letter a few days ago, but I've been so busy with finals that I didn't have a chance to call."

"Well I knew I would hear from you soon. You must be overwhelmed. Your writing is almost finished?"

"It's real close. Going to Philadelphia was a big plus. I got access to a lot of documents."

"So your pirate has done well for you."

"Privateer, Dad."

"There's little difference, no?"

Claire smiled. "I guess not. One is unofficially sanctioned."

"My daughter is going to be famous! We knew you were special the day you were born. Your mother would not be surprised at your interest in history. She wanted to name you Catherine, after the saint. I told her it was too much pressure. So we named you after her grandmother. Did you know that she was a keeper of her family's genealogy? It was a favorite hobby of hers."

Claire flashed to the memories she had of her mother pointing to old photographs in an album. They were filled with black and white portraits of men and women she never knew. They always seemed happy, and always seemed to be in a backyard or at a parade.

"I remember. It's not so different really. My pirate was an immigrant from Europe, too. Much of my research is tracing his family. I guess I didn't fall far from the tree."

"I see her more in you every day, my dear," her father said. "So, tell me about Tufts. What will you do there?"

"I'm going to shift slightly from what I'm doing now. I'll be seeking my doctorate in Feminist Studies, focused on the 18th century."

"Wonderful. Women are so strong nowadays. I remember the time when your mother bought her first pair of pants. It was quite a surprise."

Claire laughed. "Dad!"

Her father chuckled. "Yes, it was a different time. But she also had pretty legs. I hated when she covered them up."

Claire missed seeing her father regularly, and felt somewhat guilty that she called less frequently each semester. It seemed that her life was becoming more complicated, and as such, she was more distanced from the young girl she used to be. There were moments when she wished she could go back in time. To a time when her mother was alive, when they all sat in their small living room, surrounded by white lace curtains and brown paneling, and played pinochle until Carson came on TV. But in reality, she knew her father was aging quickly these days, and that time, methodically and inevitably, moved only in one direction.

"How is your hip, Daddy?"

"It's better. I have new medicine that helps."

"Is it for pain or mobility?"

"Pain, Dear. My mobile days are about over."

Claire stood up from the sofa and glanced outside. The wind had picked up. "Are you using your cane?"

"Yes, but I don't like that thing. I would prefer a wooden one. Something with more class, and maybe a brass handle. Like you see in movies."

"I'll remember that for Christmas, Dad. Are you exercising?"

"I walk two blocks every day. To Guercio's and back. To get my coffee."

"And are you eating well?" Claire asked.

"Yes, yes. Oh, did I tell you? I have new neighbors upstairs. They are Italian. A nice couple. The wife, her name is Maria, she brings me meatballs on Sundays."

"Oh that's so nice."

"Yes, they are lovely people. But soon you will come and cook for me, yes?"

"Well, I have two more weeks of school. Then I have to pack up. I'm going to live on campus in the graduate apartments at first, and they will let me move in for June. I'll only be forty minutes from you."

"I'll save my dance card for you every weekend." Her father continued, "And how is your friend Liz?"

"Oh, She's good. Frantic, like me."

"You will miss her? I know you too well, Klara. I can hear some sadness in your voice. Even with such good news."

"Yes. But she will come to Boston a lot. She likes the big city."

"Ah, this is not what you are sad about then. It is your boyfriend."

Claire paused to sip her coffee. It needed a bit more milk. She touched her necklace. It had never left her body in all the years since her mother's death. "It's complicated, Dad. He runs a restaurant. He's got his own life here — "

"Klara," her father interrupted. "Do you love him?"

Claire thought that she was prepared for this question. She knew her father would pierce through her small talk. Still, she fumbled for a moment.

"I do, Daddy. I love him."

Her father breathed deeply over the phone. "Every father waits for the day when his daughter falls in love. It is the only thing in life that matters. Does he make you happy, Dear?

"Yes. He reminds me of you, Daddy." A tear came to Claire's eye.

"And does he love you, Klara?"

"I think so."

"Then don't worry. He will not let you go without him."

Thirty-one

The day I found out began like any other. Well, slightly different in retrospect. The week prior had been out of the norm as well, making for a slight malaise in the kitchen. Diver had become quieter and kept shorter hours, absently blaming undisclosed meetings for getting behind in his prep. Something had changed. However slight, it was also bothersome, like an anxious humidity in the air.

Spring had sprung, and I took advantage of the shift in seasons by walking to the restaurant across the town. The crisp air was a welcome change from the weathered apartments that housed many Mexicans, like me and my family. Most were there only seasonally, and worked picking greens and onions from the black dirt fields surrounding the area. Because of the local agricultural economy, truckloads of migrant families created impromptu trailer parks that dotted the fields in the late spring, and again in the fall. They came to pick the corn and to wrestle with the fruit trees. They used their mattresses for storing cash. Farmers paid them by the bushel, and what money they did not save went to cerveza and bandages.

I was one of them before answering an ad in the local paper.

I arrived at *De Terre* at noon as always, even though my official hours were two to ten. My being there always saved John some time from having to wash his own *cazuelas,* and he always allowed me to make myself lunch. Sometimes he'd show me a recipe or two, and sometimes he'd let me cook something for him, like chilaquiles, which we'd eat together. That day, John entered through the back overhead door, used for deliveries, as he did when off property prior to working. He looked at me with a strange grin on his face, a mix of fear and anticipation. In his arms he carried a copy of Claire's published hardbound biography of John MacPherson.

"Morning, Bernie." He greeted.

"Good morning, Chef." I replied as always. Diver called me Bernie, though my full name is Bernardo. Bernardo Moreno. John gave me my nickname the day he hired me three years ago, when *De Terre* first opened its doors. He never called me his dishwasher. My title was always "kitchen assistant." I started immediately. I have worked with him ever since.

Diver walked over to my station, and I left the dish racks to meet him.

"How's Rosie?" he asked.

"Good, Chef. She says hello."

"And your daughter? Did she get her braces?"

"Not yet. They're going to cost four hundred dollars, even with insurance."

"That's crazy," Diver replied. "I can't believe that."

John insisted on providing health insurance for both Lanny and me. This was on top of our good wages. Years ago, when I came to this country after leaving Merida, I had very little. Though, I spoke English, which made me valuable. My wife could type. And after meeting John, I had a small piece of security. Soon thereafter, I had a daughter with lovely crooked teeth. She was my American dream.

"Blue Cross picks up fifty percent, plus the appointment cost."

"Well, her smile will be priceless."

"Yes, Chef."

"Listen, Bernie. I'm having a meeting in the dining room in half an hour. I'd like you there."

"Of course, Chef."

It was unusual that I would sit in on a meeting. In fact it was unusual that John would schedule a meeting at all. After several years with just the three of us, *De Terre* ran pretty seamlessly. We all knew what our jobs were, and what needed to be done to see the day through. In fact, *De Terre* often felt like a co-operative. The three of us each liked and admired each other. We took pride in our work. It was a place I imagined working forever. I was happy there. We were building something.

As John walked back to the line, I fumbled with a few of the last pots and pans. A large colander. A few bowls. After they were clean, I walked over to the Hobart mixer across the kitchen, re-fastening the dough hook that was dirtied earlier. The smell of bleach — for me, the smell of clean — wafted through the area close to the Alto-Shaams. I heard John wrapping food at his prep table before leaving to turn on the lights in the dining room. Ten more minutes passed lazily. After I did quick mop of the line, John pushed his head through the door and called me in.

In the dining room, I saw the poster hanging on the brick wall advertising the fundraiser for Simon's book. The reading group had been working on it for more than a month. They had decided on a mix of biographical text and photographs, several of which now dotted the brick wall of *De Terre*. One showed a young, thin Simon in his varsity jacket. Another was a wedding picture. The fundraiser was to be a concert held at the high school where he worked for most of his career. Many of his former students were coming back to play with the school's band in his honor. There was a crowdfunding website for out-of-towners. The local historical society was also involved, having helped with finding many official documents that were collated into the book. Success seemed guaranteed.

My eyes left the poster and I peered at the six-top in the middle of the room. Lanny was there, sitting beside John, along with a man in a gray suit with a stack of papers.

"Hi, Lanny," I said, extending my hand.

I could tell he was as curious as I was. "Hi, Bernie."

"Bernie," John announced, "I'd like you to meet my lawyer, Roger Brownback."

Mr. Brownback rose to greet me, and I shook his hand and nodded hello.

I sat down at the table as John offered me some coffee. A pregnant silence surrounded us, interrupted only by my spoon pinging against the ceramic mug.

John was the first to speak. "Gentlemen, I imagine you are wondering what's going on. I have some rather large news to share with you both. I'm not good at these types of things, so I'm going to say what I have to say and then Roger will follow up for me, OK?"

Lanny and I nodded.

"Lanny, you are a great friend and loyal colleague. And Bernie, you are the rock on which this place is built. As you both know, Simon's death...it hit me hard. He helped me build this place, both in spirit and in form. But now that he is gone I know that he would want me to live my life to its fullest," John paused, looking down at the table briefly. "And I've come to realize that *De Terre* was a special place for me, but ultimately it was a place for me to hide from the rest of the world. So I wanted to tell you both, here in person, that I am leaving. This will be goodbye. Now, if you will please, Roger is going to read something I've prepared. And I've got to head out for a while."

In retrospect, it seemed that we should have been more reactionary. Perhaps each of us expected the other to protest. As Lanny and I sat with jaws dropped, Mr. Brownback cleared his throat and began to read from the typed sheet of paper before him. He broke the ice because we could not.

"I, John Diver, transfer ownership of the property at 114 Travis Street, formerly known as *De Terre*, of which I am the sole proprietor, to my dear friends Lanny Alden and Bernardo

Moreno in equal partnership. The property at 114 Travis Street will be known from this moment on as *The Family Kitchen*."

I was slow to wrap my head around what I had heard.

"Wait. What?" Lanny asked, incredulously.

"Congratulations, gentlemen," answered Mr. Brownback. "This restaurant is yours. You are each going to need a lawyer. We will need to sign some papers and agree to terms to make it official, but in essence, you are now equal part owners."

Slowly, wondrously, our reality set in. Mr. Brownback filled in the details. We learned that Simon had left John an inheritance, and that the property mortgage was paid off. We would be leasing the building in perpetuity for a modest monthly sum. We were left complete creative control.

We talked about renovations. We talked about business plans. I called my wife to celebrate. Lanny and I spent the next several hours drawing up ideas on paper placemats. By the end of the afternoon, Lanny and I were having drinks at the bar in celebration, not even realizing that John had not returned and that a sign had been placed at the front door declaring "Under New Ownership." We looked at each other as though waking up from a dream. Soon, parents and their children would become our new clients. Old friends would move away and on with their lives. We wondered if we would ever see John again. But somehow we knew he was not coming back. This was his goodbye.

The reader may wonder why I have not introduced myself before now, why I hid in the background of this writing until the end of this story. You see, this is a story of many stories. It is a story of a privateer. It is the story of a schoolteacher. It is the story of a people and their place in history. But most of all, it is a story of a man and a woman. Why bother with superfluous details? The best observer is the invisible one. And I have tried to remain thus.

The sunlight grew lower as it streamed through the window shades. The first early breezes of summer were ushering in a transformation. The limbs of the maple trees were gravid with the weight of their new leaves, which spread out like green fingers across the skies. The honeybees were picking over every flower busily. The western hills stayed lit a little more each day. I imagined my neighbors in the fields with baskets of crisp white onions, covered by the sweet smell of humus, digging the earth from beneath their fingernails. Back at that six-top, Lanny and I daydreamed with our arms cradled behind our heads in ecstatic consummation. Soon, my wife, Rosaria, arrived with little Tessie. I knew that I would miss her crooked smile the hour after it was straightened.

As Lanny stood and reached for the Espolon one final time, he noticed an envelope tacked behind us at the bar mirror. We toasted to *The Family Kitchen* and each downed a final shot. Then Lanny opened the note. Inside was a photo of John and Claire and a forwarding address in Boston. Three stories had been written. One was still unfolding. Mine was next.

~~~

About the Author

Darryl Lauster is an Associate Professor of Art at the University of Texas at Arlington, an award-winning artist and sculptor, and published writer. His work is based in the research of American history and mythology, and utilizes digital media, printmaking, sculpture and installation. He won a Joan Mitchell Foundation Grant for Painters and Sculptors in 2010, and he has also received grants from the Peter Reed Foundation, the Netherland-America Foundation and the Houston Arts Alliance.

His visual work can be found in the permanent collections of the Philadelphia Museum of Art, The University of Texas at Arlington, McNeese State University and the Museum of Fine Arts Houston. Lauster's written work can be found in The Conversation, Gulf Coast Magazine, and Artlies Magazine.

Learn more at www.darryllauster.com.

RITES OF PASSAGE
is also available as an e-book
for Kindle, Amazon Fire, iPad, Nook,
Kobo and Android e-readers.
Visit creatorspublishing.com to learn more.

o o o

CREATORS PUBLISHING

We publish books.
We find compelling storytellers and
help them craft their narrative,
distributing their novels and collections
worldwide.

o o o

www.ingramcontent.com/pod-product-compliance
Lightning Source LLC
Chambersburg PA
CBHW051257250626
47155CB00009B/3330